"Child Executive Officer "

(CEO)

R.A. POWELL

First Published in 2019 by Blossom Spring Publishing

ISBN 978-1-9161735-5-2

E: admin@blossomspringpublishing.com

W: www.blossomspringpublishing.com

Also by R.A Powell…

Odd Socks was a finalist in The People's Book Prize 2018 and is available at Amazon, Waterstones, Barnes & Noble and more…

 r.a.powell27

 ra_powell27

 rpowellauthor

www.robertpowell-author.com

For Mam and for anyone who has lost someone they love.

xxx

Chapter One

Before we begin, I would like to assure you that for most children, the transition from primary to secondary school is a mostly positive and wonderful experience. For some children however, it can be brutal and harrowing which was sadly the case for Ben Hamley, who had just started **King Admiral Old Boys School**, the most prestigious school in the country.

From the outside, King Admiral was a truly magnificent building; with Tudor-style brickwork, luscious grounds, and world-class sports facilities; King Admiral was a symbol of excellence. It was so prestigious that seven Prime Ministers, three Nobel Peace Prize Winners, and hundreds of leading scientists, doctors, and academics had attended the school through the years. It was the kind of place where Michelin Star Chefs prepared the school dinners and Olympic athletes delivered the PE lessons. If you secured a place at King Admiral, you really were made for life.

However, you've probably heard the saying 'never judge a book by its cover'. Well this certainly rang true of King Admiral; because if you ever had the misfortune of setting foot inside this wonderful piece of architecture, you would quickly come to realise that the place was rotten to its core. Like an apple left in the blistering sun for hours on end, the school was infested with rotten, nasty and creepy maggots. And that was just the teachers. For Ben, their spitefulness had drained every last drop of beauty from this awe-inspiring building.

Even though his parents were rich, young Ben wasn't spoilt. And he certainly wasn't a brat. His parents had made their fortune from humble beginnings and had instilled in Ben the importance of kindness and hard work. A sensitive soul, Ben had worked extra hard to get into King Admiral. You see Ben was dyslexic, and due to the extraordinary lengths that their only child had gone to, in order to pass the admissions test, his Mum and Dad were the proudest parents in the world.

Now just six weeks into his new school, sitting through yet another exam, Ben felt a deep sadness in the pit of his stomach. You see King Admiral was obsessed with two things; sports and exams; the worst possible combination for a short and skinny dyslexic boy who wasn't very good at either. And because Ben was always the last to be picked out on the field, he was immediately deemed an outcast. The rugby team dunked his head down the toilet. The football lads called him **'Big Ben'** (Ben was *really* small) and hid his pants and trousers after practice. One time they tied him to the goalposts at lunchtime and left him there all afternoon. And the teachers, they were worse than the boys; horrible ghastly creatures with cigarette-stained fingers and poisonous honky breath that smelled like a duvet soaked in cheap coffee.

It had been playing on the young boy's mind that he needed to tell his parents just how miserable he was at school. The trouble was that they were *so happy* that he was there. As he sat hunched at the back of class, trying to make sense of the pointless questions on the exam paper in front him, his brain started to bubble away like an egg in a hot pan. He knew he had to tell his parents how he felt when they returned from their charity expedition in Alaska. Lifting his head, he glanced around the musty classroom and sighed at the sight of his classmates; heads down and deep in concentration. Their deathly silence fueling his anger like petrol on a flame. He rubbed his head in frustration…

What does this mean? It's complete nonsense! What is the point in learning this?

4m2/4567;-)88 x

f5E123LOL =

The door burst open. "Benjamin Hamley, come to the Headmaster's office immediately."

Ben's cherub face reddened. "But...but...what have I done sir?"

Could he hear me thinking? I only said the question was nonsense!

"And grab your bag and coat, you won't be coming back today."

Chapter Two

Ben furiously grabbed his bag and skateboard. As he trudged down to the front of class, he felt a foot slide out and catch his ankle...**CRASH!** Ben hurtled forwards, landing face-first on the dusty classroom floor, his bag and skateboard clattering to the ground.

"HA HA HA HA HA!" his classmates cackled.

"CLASSIC!" someone shouted.

Ben gritted his teeth and picked himself up. He licked his lips and tasted a metallic flavour that had sadly become so familiar to him these last six weeks. Wiping the blood from his mouth, he spotted Vince Howler, his worst enemy, grinning like the Joker from Batman. "Big Ben - Ding Dong!" he sniggered.

Ben felt his bottom lip wobble.

"Come on Benjamin, hurry up. We haven't got all day," the teacher shouted.

"But...but...sir..."

"But sir nothing...come on will you," huffed Mr Furrilip.

Mr Furrilip was Ben's least favourite teacher, and in a place like King Admiral, that was saying something. Mr Furrilip was very tall; six foot ten-and-a-half inches to be precise. In fact, he was six foot eleven inches on a windy day if he forgot to brush his thinning hair. Ben knew this because Mr Furrilip frequently reminded everyone of his incredible tallness. He would often use his height to emphasis the size of pretty much anything.

He could be teaching Geography class about insects…

"…did you know that I'm 35 times taller than a grasshopper."

Or Mathematics class…

"...the square root of 34,225 is 185 which is precisely the same height as I am in centimetres."

He was also extremely skinny. As in *wafer-thin-ham-skinny.* When he walked, his legs and arms wobbled like *Cheestrings.* His biggest fault however wasn't the fact that he didn't like Ben and he would embarrass the young boy about being dyslexic, or that when he wobbled down the corridor his shoes would squelch due to his feet oozing with sweat. No, it wasn't any of those things. Mr Furrilip's biggest fault was his moustache. It was quite possibly the most enormous moustache *ever* grown. Quite easily the size of an **overweight** hamster. Its size however, wasn't the problem. The real issue was its ability to attract leftover food whenever the man ate. Mr Furrilip's monstrous moustache was simply a haven for food. A food magnet if you will. Almost every day, Ben would notice a soggy cornflake, a dried-up piece of sweetcorn, or some other solitary crumb of left-over food dangling from it. Sometimes when he was shouting at Ben, the food would dance and wiggle in time with the movement of his mouth. On other occasions, it actually looked as if the food was trying to escape in search of a better life. But the poor left-over food never stood a chance; Mr Furrilip's moustache was like Velcro, nothing could escape. Ben often wondered if that was the reason why the man was so skinny, because the food never made it past his moustache.

Alone in the corridor with him, Ben noticed that Mr Furrilip had eaten mashed potato for lunch. "Dear boy, look at the state of you," he barked. "Go to the toilets and clean yourself up." A dollop of crusty mash fell from his bushy lip and landed on Ben's shoe. "Then come straight to Miss Cruncher's office. NOW HURRY!"

After cleaning himself up and grabbing a handful of toilet paper to hold over his swollen nose, Ben traipsed down the corridor to Miss Cruncher's office, the place that everyone in school tried their best to avoid. Almost as tall as Mr Furrilip, but at least twenty times his width, **Miss Cruncher** was a **brute** of a woman. She *ate* 100 cigarettes a day and judging by her deep raspy voice it was safe to say she probably smoked a similar number too.

Holding the toilet roll over his nose, Ben pushed the door open and nervously peered inside. "Uncle Mike, what are you doing here?"

"Sit down Ben," replied Mike, nodding to the vacant chair next to him.

Miss Cruncher was slumped behind her desk, surrounded by piles of papers and chewed-up cigarettes; her blister-like face expressionless.

"What is it?" asked Ben as he took a seat.

Uncle Mike fidgeted. "It's your Mum and Dad...I don't know how to say this..." He stared at his bony hands. "They've...erm...they've gone."

"What do you mean… they've gone?" asked Ben, feeling warm suddenly.

Mike stared blankly into space. "They've gone Ben…they've…erm…died."

Ben's tummy performed a somersault twist, like he'd just eaten a mountain of out-of-date Brussel Sprouts before riding the fastest rollercoaster in the world without a seatbelt. His body turned weak and floppy. He felt boiling hot suddenly. He dropped the toilet roll from his nose releasing a fresh stream of blood onto his shirt. "But…but…what do you mean?"

"They've gone Ben..."

Ben’s heart pounded in his chest, his head was spinning. "But I thought they were in Alaska? I spoke to them yesterday. How can they be dead?"

"They were eaten by a polar bear," replied Mike under his breath.

"Eaten by a polar bear? But...but..."

Miss Cruncher intervened. “Benjamin Hamley, why don't you go home; your uncle will take you."

Ben glanced at his uncle and whispered, "Uncle Mike, will you take me home?"

Chapter Three

Relieved to be home, Ben’s mind was muddled, more like scrambled eggs this time. Uncle Mike hadn't said a word to him in the car on the way home. This didn’t surprise Ben as his uncle had never said much to him anyway, even when his parents were alive. He had never liked his Dad’s brother. There was always some get-rich-quick-scheme which ended up with either Mike lying or begging Ben’s Dad for money. Most of the time it was both. His uncle always lied, even when it was plainly obvious to everyone else that he wasn’t telling the truth. And even after all of the evidence pointed to the fact that he was lying, he would still not admit defeat. Like a secret spy held captive by terrorists, he would stick to his guns and not admit the truth. You had to admire his resilience if anything. Unbeknown to Ben, a few months ago his uncle was caught stealing a teddy bear from *Toy Co*, his Mum and Dad’s toy store. When he was spotted on CCTV by Cyril the security guard, and the footage was shown to him, Mike still denied it. He explained that it was someone else who looked just like him. When Cyril asked, *"...can I ask why a 42 years old man is stealing a teddy bear?"* Mike simply replied, *"...I don't know Cyril, you'll have to ask my lookalike."* But despite his constant lies and sneaky behavior, Ben's Dad had always given him the benefit of the doubt.

The young boy closed the front door. He was welcomed by a soothing and familiar voice. "Oh my baby Ben, come here and give your Auntie Mo a big cuddle."

Ben opened his arms and let his auntie wrap him into her.

Auntie Mo wasn't Ben's *real* auntie, but she was an auntie in every other way. She was funny, kind, caring and the best cook. She was short and plump with a sweet tooth and the chubbiest ankles you've ever seen. Her soft Scottish accent hummed like a songbird and she fussed over Ben like he was her own son. Auntie Mo was technically a live-in maid, she had worked for the Hamley's for 20 years as a cook and nanny. Her husband died 12 years ago and Ben and his parents were all she had.

Now Ben was all she had.

Her kind face was flushed red. "I can't believe the news poppet, it's terrible," she said as he nestled into her (*Mo rarely called Ben by his actual name*). "How about I make you a big mug of my special hot chocolate? Are you hungry?"

Ben was calm. He was numb. He didn't feel emotional in the slightest. "How come I'm not upset Mo? I haven't cried yet."

"Oh poppet, you're in shock that's why. It's so much to take in," she sniffled.

"Does that make me a horrible person for not crying?" he asked, peering up at Mo from the comfort of her arms.

Ben's head shook as his auntie let out an almighty sob. "It does not my beautiful boy, you are the most gorgeous and thoughtful person so don't you feel bad about not crying." She took in a deep breath. "You will grieve when the time is right."

"A special hot chocolate would be lovely Mo."

*** CEO ***

The next two weeks went by in a blink. Lots of people visited Ben's house; friends, neighbours, people to arrange the funeral, employees from his Mum and Dad's company. Other than occasionally playing in the garden on his beloved skateboard, Ben stayed in his room most of the time. Mo would bring him a mug of hot chocolate and a big plate of his favourite food; bangers 'n mash. Every night he would lay in bed thinking about his Mum and Dad. He would remember playing hide and seek with them. Or the time when he got his head stuck in the garden fence and his Dad rubbed butter over Ben's ears to yank him out, only to be then attacked by a swarm of bees who were craving the sweet butter. Ben would sometimes smile to himself when he reminisced about his parents but he didn't cry once.

The funeral went smoothly. Ben kept himself quiet throughout. He didn't feel like speaking to anyone and it was all a bit of a blur. There was however, one thing that stuck in his mind. Outside the cemetery, he noticed two extremely large men hovering near the gates. Despite it being a cloudy day, they were wearing sunglasses, and there was something about them which made Ben shiver as he entered the church.

Chapter Four

Now that his parents had been laid to rest and the house was less busy with visitors, it had dawned on Ben that everyone around him was getting on with their lives.

"When would you like to go back to school poppet?" Mo said one morning while making breakfast.

The word 'school' made his stomach churn. "I don't want to go back Mo - the teachers stink! They are horrible! And the other boys pick on me. I hate it. I'm not going."

She brought a plate of toast to the table. "But you're eleven years old my dear! If you don't go to school what will you do? How about we try another school?"

The phone rang.

"Let me get that..." said Mo.

Ben buttered a slice of toast as Mo answered.

"Hello there…"

“Ah, ok...”

“...right I had never thought about that...”

“...no I'm not related to Ben...”

“*...but I have lived with the family for over 20 years...*”

“...there's only his Uncle Mike...”

“...ok then, I'll arrange for him to call you...”

“...yes...and you...bye."

Mo returned to the table.

"Who was that Mo?" asked Ben as he took a slurp of orange juice.

Mo took a seat. "Well dear...I guess you'll need to find out sooner or later...it was your Mum and Dad's lawyer. We need to arrange the inheritance."

"What does inheritance mean?"

Mo poured him more orange juice. "It means when someone dies, they leave all of their possessions, such as a house or a car, and all of their money to a loved one - usually their children."

"What do they want with Uncle Mike?" asked Ben.

Mo sighed. "Well, your uncle is very sadly the only family relation you have left. Because he's an adult and you're under the age of 18, he is now classified as your legal guardian. He will have to speak to the lawyer to arrange everything."

"But I want you involved Mo. You may not be my real auntie but you're the best auntie anyone could ever wish for."

Mo burst into tears.

Chapter Five

"Come on Ben, we're going to be late," Mike called impatiently.

"I'm coming!" hollered Ben as he bounced down the stairs, his skateboard tucked under his arm.

Leaning against the bannister at the bottom of the stairs, Mike looked every inch the wheeler and dealer. With his super expensive suit, shiny pink tie with white polka dots, over-sized gold watch, and his thinning hair brushed tightly back across his scrawny head, he was the epitome of a dodgy businessman. “Why are you bringing that thing?” he scowled, glancing at the skateboard. “We’re going to meet the Family lawyer not to see your mates.”

“I don’t have any mates,” huffed Ben, brushing past him.

"Well you can leave it in the car,” he shouted as Ben headed straight for the door. He straightened his tie and stopped Ben in his tracks. “Now listen, when we get to the lawyer's office, just sit and be quiet will you. Just let me do the talking."

"Ok Uncle Mike, whatever you say," replied Ben, gripping his skateboard extra tightly.

*** CEO ***

Outside the lawyer’s office, Ben gasped as he climbed out of the car and peered up at the towering glass building. People in fancy suits were dashing in and out of the revolving doors, coffee in one hand, phone in the other. Ben and Mike walked up to the building and were just about to enter when they heard a deep gravelly voice. “LOOK WHO IT IS TERRY! FANCY BUMPIN’ INTO MIKE HAMLEY OUTSIDE A LAWYER’S OFFICE!”

Ben couldn’t believe it. It was the same men who were outside the cemetery at his Mum and Dad’s funeral!

Mike tensed up. “Oh...hi...Gruff...great to see you…what are you doing here?”

Built like an American fridge, Gruff had razor-like stubble and a neck that blended seamlessly into his back. He gave a hearty cackle, his red cheeks glowing. “Just enjoyin’ the fresh air Mike, that’s all,” he growled, a mouthful of frothy spit splattering onto Mike’s super expensive suit. “Just ya’ make sure that ya’ come to see us soon eh? We’ve missed ya’ Mike. ‘aven’t we Terry?”

“Yeah, we miss ya’ a lot Mike. Keep in touch won’t ya Mikey boy,” boomed Terry, who was built like a slightly smaller American fridge. He blew a kiss and gave a throaty laugh, his multiple chins wobbled.

“Ok fellas, I’ll see you soon. I’ll be in touch,” said Mike with a forceful cheer. And with that, he spun round and quickly pushed through the revolving doors.

Something gave Ben the impression that Gruff and Terry didn’t miss Mike at all.

Chapter Six

Inside the lawyer's office, it was even more spectacular. Lights glistened on the cream marble floor and fancy sculptures were dotted about the huge reception area. Although there were lots of people milling around, it still looked empty. Ben immediately regretted leaving his skateboard in the car, this would be the perfect place for it! "Who are Gruff and Terry?" he asked, running to keep up with his uncle.

"None of your business Ben, just a couple of old friends from school. Come on, we're going to be late."

They approached a large desk where an old man was sat reading the newspaper.

"We're here to see Mrs Weston," said Mike, glancing over his shoulder. No doubt to check if Gruff and Terry had followed them.

The man peered up and removed his spectacles. "Tissue?"

“Sorry?” asked Mike.

The man held out a tissue. “Would you like one? I think a bird has pooed on your suit!”

Mike glanced at his shoulder. “Oh that, yes thanks.” He grabbed the tissue and wiped Gruff’s spit from his suit.

“That’s better,” smiled the old man. “Now apologies, who did you say you were here to see?”

“We’re here to see Mrs Weston,” replied Mike, leaning on the counter.

“We?” asked the man.

“Yes, me and Ben,” said Mike irritably.

“Ben?” asked the old man.

“Yes Ben Hamley… and I’m Mike Hamley.”

“I can see that Mr Hamley but where is this Ben?”

“Here,” replied Mike, nodding to his nephew.

“Where?” asked the man.

“Down here!” cried Ben.

The man put his glasses on and leaned over the counter. “Ah young man, sorry about that, I couldn’t see you there!” he smiled. “Welcome both, Mrs Weston is waiting for you. Please take the lift to the 27th floor.”

Chapter Seven

PING! The lift doors opened and Ben followed his uncle down a long corridor. People were dashing in and out of rooms, carrying large files of paperwork, and generally looking important. A lady appeared in a striking navy blue suit with large gold buttons. "Hello!" she waved enthusiastically. "Good morning Mr Hamley," she smiled. "And good morning Ben, I'm Penelope Weston, Attorney at Law."

A superstar lawyer with a Hollywood smile, shiny dark hair, bright red lips, and skyscraper heels, Penelope Weston spoke a million miles an hour as she led them into her plush office with panoramic views of the city centre. "Take a seat the both of you, can I get you anything?"

"Erm… a coffee would be lovely," said Mike as he sat down.

"Excellent, what type of coffee would you like?" smiled Mrs Weston, taking a seat behind a large oak desk. Without pausing for breath, she reeled off the coffee menu with impressive speed and precision, "we've got *Cappuccino, Iced, Americano, Espresso, Macchiato, Mocha, Latte, Forest-Fire-Flat-White, Slim-Jim-Vanilla-Bean, Skinny-Mini-Mocha-Locha, Creamy-Dreamy-Caramel or Choco-Coconut-Cloud-With-Room-Temperature-Foam.*"

"…erm…just coffee from a jar will do," replied Mike.

Mrs Weston struggled to hide her distaste. "Coffee *from a jar*? Well ok then…if that's what you want… coffee from a jar it is." She wrote this down on a notepad. "Do you take milk?"

"Yes please," said Mike.

"Mmm," said Mrs Weston, writing this down as well. "So that's coffee from a jar with milk. What type of milk? We have *Almond, Soya, Coconut, Rice, Hemp, Flax, Cashew, Oat or Goat*."

"Erm…do you have *normal* milk?" asked Mike.

"From a cow?" shrieked Mrs Weston, taken aback.

"Yes please, cow's milk," smiled Mike.

Mrs Weston squirmed, she clearly disapproved of Mike's taste in coffee. "Ok then…would you like that full fat, semi-skimmed or skimmed?"

"Full fat please," said Mike, fidgiting slightly.

Mrs Weston gave him a judgemental look. “Well ok then…if you’re sure that’s what you really want…do you take sugar?”

“Yes, two please,” fidgeted Mike.

“Good gosh!” cried Mrs Weston. “Well…two sugars it is.” She jotted this down. “Ok, so what type of sugar? We have *White, Brown, Sweeteners, Agave-Nectar, Coconut, Honey, Date-Paste, Stevia-Extracts or Monk-Fruit*.”

Mike hesitated. “Erm...I think I’ll…” He looked to his nephew for help. Ben ignored him and enjoyed a private chuckle at Mike’s bamboozlement.

Mrs Weston glanced at her watch. “So what is it going to be Mr Hamley?” she asked hurriedly. “As you know, a lawyer’s time is money! I charge by the hour you know!”

Mike sighed. “Just two white sugars please.”

"And Ben, what about you?" she smiled.

"Please can I have a lemonade Mrs Weston?" asked Ben, admiring the views behind her.

"Of course!" She pressed a button on her desk which buzzed through to her secretary. "Sandra darling, can you fetch some coffee and lemonade please."

“Of course Mrs Weston, what type of coffee?” replied Sandra through the speaker.

The lawyer’s face tightened. “Coffee from a jar with milk.”

“From a jar?” came the reply. “But we don’t…”

“Just find some please Sandra,” interrupted Mrs Weston, half-smiling at Mike and Ben.

“What type of milk?” came the reply.

“Cow’s milk,” said Mrs Weston through gritted teeth.

“Sugar?”

“Two,” replied the lawyer, glancing at Mike.

“Any preference on the sugar?” asked Sandra.

“Just *normal* white sugar please,” sighed Mrs Weston, tapping her fingers on the desk.

“Ok Mrs Weston, anything else?”

“Oh yes actually Sandra, please can I have my mid-morning smoothie?” she asked enthusiastically.

“No problem,” replied Sandra. “Is that cabbage-banana-avocado-tofu-rhubarb-ginger-lemongrass-cinnamon and apple?”

Mrs Weston pulled a face. “Sandra darling, now you know that cabbage-banana-avocado-tofu-rhubarb-ginger-lemongrass-cinnamon and apple is my *early morning smoothie*.” She glanced at Mike and Ben. “Sandra sweetie, my *mid-morning smoothie* is mango-kale-coconut-charcoal-beetroot-pineapple-grasshopper-purple broccoli and blueberry.”

“Ah of course Mrs Weston, your drinks will be with you shortly.”

“Ok thank you Sandra darling… toodlepip!”

Putting her designer glasses on and shuffling some paperwork, Mrs Weston checked her watch and smiled. “Right, let’s get down to business. I have a 12.00 meeting so let’s make this quick.”

Chapter Eight

"First of all, please can I offer my deepest condolences to you both. I couldn't believe it when I heard the news." Mrs Weston leaned forward and removed her glasses. "I have known Mr and Mrs Hamley for over 20 years." She leaned back in her chair and sighed. "I hadn't seen them for a while. And Ben, I remember you when you were a little baby," she smiled. "I simply don't know what to say other than I'm incredibly shocked and saddened at the news. I can't imagine how you both must be feeling."

"Thank you Mrs Weston," replied Ben.

"Please, call me Penelope," she smiled warmly.

"Thank you Penelope," said Ben.

"Yes it's been a terrible shock…erm …Penelope, so thank you for your kind words," added Mike.

Penelope offered a gentle smile. “Well if there’s anything I can do please let me know.” She put her glasses on and shuffled her paperwork again. “Now, the reason you’re both here is because Mr and Mrs Hamley had already transferred their estate into a trust fund.” She swept her long dark hair from her face. “Why? Because they have one of the best lawyers in town,” she chuckled. “But also Ben, you are the sole beneficiary of your parents’ estate…”

“Excuse me?” spat Mike, almost leaping from his chair.

“Sorry Mike, you have a question?” replied Penelope, removing her glasses.

“Erm…yes…yes…I do have a question...” said Mike, shifting in his seat, “you said Ben is the sole beneficiary of the estate, is that correct?”

Penelope placed her glasses on the tip of her nose. “It is indeed Mike, apologies if I wasn’t clear. Ben will become the sole owner of the estate which includes the family property portfolio, all possessions, cash in the bank, investments and of course the family business *Toy Co."*

"Erm...well ok then..." stammered Mike.

"What's a Trust Fund and what does sole beneficiary mean?" asked Ben.

"Good question sweetie," smiled Penelope. "Think of a Trust Fund as a very special bank account for parents to pass on their money to their children." She fiddled a pen with her fingers. "And sole beneficiary means you Ben. You are the sole beneficiary, the one and only person who will now own all of your parents' wealth."

Ben glanced at his uncle. "So does this mean I also own Toy Co?"

Penelope leaned back in her leather chair. "It does indeed Ben, of course you are too young to do anything but as it was a family business owned by your parents then you are now the owner." She glanced at Mike. "Now your uncle, in his position as Legal

Guardian, will be in charge of your Trust Fund until your 18th birthday."

"And what does that mean exactly?" asked Mike irritably.

Penelope flipped the pen round her fingers. "What it means Mike is that you will be the main contact regarding the financial performance of Toy Co, and day-to-day management of finances such as property, bills and other fees."

"Mum was the boss of Toy Co - who will do that now?" queried Ben.

“Well, I have been in charge of Toy Co for the last 12 months,” said Mike forcefully. “Does that change things?”

Penelope looked at Ben. "Well young man, as your uncle has *temporarily* been in charge, you may want to keep it that way for the time being. But of course, you could hire a new CEO if you wanted to,” she explained. “But your uncle will need to do that on your behalf along with the Board of Directors of Toy

Co."

"So just how big is this Trust Fund?" asked Mike. "I mean, what exactly have they left?"

Penelope stood up as her secretary entered with a tray of drinks. "Ah splendid, thank you Sandra. Just leave them here on the desk." Penelope served Mike his coffee and poured Ben his lemonade. "That's a good question Mike," said Penelope while handing them both a piece of paper. "You can see the full list of assets and investments listed in this document." She took a slurp of her mango-kale-coconut-charcoal-beetroot-pineapple-grasshopper-purple broccoli and blueberry smoothie. "In short Ben, your parents have left you one heck of a legacy."

*** CEO ***

In the car on the way home, Mike pulled his silent act again. Ben asked him about Gruff and Terry but his uncle just brushed the topic aside. So Ben stared out of the window and thought about Toy Co. His Mum and Dad had started the business from nothing and now it was one of the biggest toy companies in the world.

He tried to read the document that Penelope had given him but he found it difficult. Although Ben had come to terms with being dyslexic a long time ago, it was at times like this when he became frustrated because he really wanted to be able to read what was on the paper. Being dyslexic meant that it took Ben a lot longer than most people to read books, magazines, or instructions. The words and numbers on the page appear all jumbled up which makes it a lot harder to understand. He looked at Mike who was staring blankly out of the window. Ben sighed. He would ask Mo to read it with him when he returned home.

Chapter Nine

After deciding not to tell Mo about Gruff and Terry, the two dodgy men outside Penelope's office, Ben opened the door, he was glad to be home. "Mo, I'm home!"

"Hello my darling," replied Mo, her plump face lighting up. "You want a cookie? I've just baked them."

"That would be wonderful," beamed Ben. "I need you to help me read some information."

"Of course my dear, let me pour you a glass of orange and fetch the cookies," she said brightly. "Where is your uncle?"

"He's gone straight home," shrugged Ben. He took a seat at the breakfast bar. "He barely spoke to me all morning."

Mo returned with two glasses of orange and plate of warm chocolate chip cookies. "How did it go at the lawyer's office?" she asked.

"It was good, Mrs Weston was very kind and helpful," said Ben. "She gave me this." Ben slid the paper to Mo. "I need you to help me read it."

Mo put her glasses on. "Now let me see." Ben took an enthusiastic bite of a cookie as Mo read the document in silence. After a few moments, she started to cry.

"What's the matter Mo?" the boy said putting his arm around her.

"Oh I'm sorry poppet," wept Mo. "It's just your Mum and Dad were such fantastic people. They worked so hard…" She blew her nose. "…and they've left you an awful lot." She slid the paper back to Ben. "Right, now let me help you read this."

Over the years, Mo had been a tremendous support to Ben to improve his reading. She would often sit with Ben and his parents and the three of them would help him understand and recognise the different sounds that make up words. And now, without his Mum and Dad around, it was just the two of them, sat at the kitchen table as they read the paper. Ben was shocked to discover that his Mum and Dad had left him an astonishing legacy…

- £48million cash in the bank
- 20-bedroom family home in the UK including all possessions – valued at £25millon
- Holiday homes in Italy, New Zealand, Morocco, Hawaii and Brazil including all possessions – valued at £15million
- Toy Co (the company his parents founded) – valued at £300million
- Stocks and shares valued at £1.2billion
- Toy Co Charitable Foundation
- 24 cars and automobiles
- One Yacht
- One aeroplane
- One speedboat
- Four horses and stables
- 2.5 Unicorns (*ok, well maybe that's not actually true*)

Ben almost fell from his chair. "Wow," he said rubbing his eyes. "I always knew we were wealthy but I didn't know we were that rich!"

He would do anything to bring his parents back. And even more so now that he could see how hard they had worked at building Toy Co from a tiny high street shop to one of the biggest toy companies in the world.

"Your Mum and Dad were amazing people," whispered Mo with watery eyes. "They were so successful." She placed her hand on Ben's and looked at him. "But more importantly darling, they were kind and caring people. I'll never forget how supportive they were to me when my dear Alfred passed away 12 years ago." Tears slid down her plump cheeks. "They were so lovely."

Ben looked at Mo and hugged her. "And you are doing exactly the same for me right now."

Mo burst into tears.

Again.

Chapter Ten

At 3pm the next day, Ben sat at the back of Geography class, thinking to himself that maybe Mo was right, maybe it was a good idea to come back to school after all (Mo was *always right*). Maybe one small upside of losing your parents is that the bullies leave you alone; no one had called him any names, even Vince Howler had been strangely quiet. Mr Furrilip hadn't said a word to him either. Now you could think that as a teacher, Mr Furrilip would have a duty of care to speak to Ben on his first day back after such a tragic and life-changing event. But he hadn't, and to Ben this was a good thing, because he didn't really want to see what the man had eaten for lunch.

"Before we finish," announced Mr Furrilip, jabbing his long spindly finger at the wall, where a world map was displayed. "Next week, we will be learning about Alaska."

Ben's heart jolted. *Was this some kind of twisted joke?* He eagerly eyed Mr Furrilip's face to detect any sign of callousness but there was nothing. He glanced at Vince Howler who was staring straight back at him wearing that evil smirk.

Mr Furrilip continued, "Alaska is a fascinating place, one of the few parts of the world that has glaciers, snow, earthquakes, and volcanoes, so there is a lot to cover. Does anyone know where Alaska is?"

Vince raised his hand. "Benjamin will know sir," he smirked. "He knows all about Alaska don't you Benjamin?"

The whole class turned to face Ben. He felt his face redden.

"Well Benjamin, do you know where Alaska is?" Mr Furrilip asked impatiently.

A few moments of silence passed before Ben cleared his throat. "The United States of America sir," he said quietly.

"Yes Benjamin… that is… correct. Alaska is in the United States of America," replied Mr Furrilip, visibly annoyed that Ben had answered correctly.

Ben was furious. Only three weeks ago, his parents had tragically died in Alaska. This must be a huge coincidence. Surely Mr Furrilip wasn't that mean? But why is Vince laughing?

Vince raised his hand again. "Sir, will we be studying bears as well? There are lots of bears in Alaska."

It was now obvious to Ben that Vince was well aware of the connection. And like some of the world's deadliest predators, the school bully exploited any sign of weakness in his prey.

"Good question Vince, bears and other wildlife will certainly form part of the lesson," answered Mr Furrilip brightly.

Vince gave Ben a sly look. "Excellent sir, it's just that bears are my favourite animal. Such powerful creatures..."

Vince's cronies sniggered.

Ben swallowed hard. He wanted to say something, but he was too shocked. How could anyone be so cruel? He felt himself getting hotter and hotter. His blood was practically boiling. He sighed with relief when the bell rang.

"Right, that's enough class. See you next week," called Mr Furrilip.

*** CEO ***

"How was your first day back poppet?" asked Mo as Ben walked through the door.

The young boy usually told his auntie everything. However, his experience in Geography class had left him in a state of shock. He didn't want to worry her. "Yeah it was fine Mo, I'm glad I went back. I'm just heading upstairs to get changed."

Chapter Eleven

By the weekend, Ben had put Vince and the Geography lesson behind him. Out shopping with Mo, he felt a sudden wave of excitement. “Mo, please can we go to Toy Co?” he asked as they ambled down the high street.

“Of course dear, you own it after all!” she chuckled. The pair smiled to themselves as they continued past the rows of shops and market stalls when Ben spotted a group of boys outside an amusement arcade. He grabbed Mo’s arm and moved closer to the group, blending into the crowds of shoppers.

“Where are you going dear?” asked Mo.

“I’ll tell you in a minute Mo, just follow me.”

He led her to a shop window, just a few feet away from the group of boys. Turning his back and eavesdropping on their conversation, Ben heard a familiar voice. “My stupid Dad, he never turns up to anything. He missed my footy match again this morning."

"Who is it Ben?" asked Mo.

"Shush!" whispered Ben. "Stand here with me a second."

Ben recognised the voice. How could he not? It was the unmistakable hiss of Vince Howler. He listened as Vince continued, "he never takes any interest in me. I got into trouble at school last week and he just shrugged. The man is useless."

As Vince continued to complain about his Dad, Ben listened with intent. It suddenly dawned him why Vince is such a horrible person. His behaviour is obviously a cry for help to get his Dad's attention.

"Who are we listening to Ben?" asked Mo, growing slightly impatient.

Ben smiled. "Oh no one Mo, just someone from school. Come on, let's go and visit Toy Co!"

Keeping his head down to avoid being spotted by Vince, Ben grabbed Mo's hand and led her down the high street until they reached the iconic store. Its famous 'Toy Co' sign, glittering with flashing stars in rainbow colours, hung proudly above the mesmerising window displays. It was a logo that was etched in the memory of millions of children across the world. Ben stopped again and grabbed his auntie's arm. "Why are there lots of people sleeping outside the shops Mo? Are they ok?"

Surprised that Ben wasn't focused on the incredible toy store that he now owned, Mo put her arm around him. "Oh poppet, those poor people are homeless. They have nowhere to live so they have to sleep on the streets."

Homelessness had increased dramatically in recent years. Ben could vaguely remember his Mum and Dad donating money to a homeless charity once. However, he was very young back then and had never truly understood what being homeless had really meant. Now that Mo had explained it to him, it made him sad. And angry.

"That's terrible!" cried Ben, shivering slightly. "Surely we can help them? We've got loads of space in our house. And loads of money. It's getting cold now.

We could take them in, and you could cook them some of your delicious food?"

"My dear, you are such a sweet boy," smiled Mo, gripping his hand tightly. "But people are homeless for a lot of different reasons. It's a very complicated issue." She nodded to Toy Co. "Why don't we go inside and afterwards we'll buy them some food? Then we can talk more about it when we get home. How does that sound?"

"Ok Mo, that sounds good."

Chapter Twelve

Ben had always felt a huge sense of pride whenever he visited his Mum and Dad's toy store. However, this time it was different with it being the first time he had set foot inside Toy Co since they had passed away. A pang of sadness stuck in his chest as he pushed through the revolving doors. A sweet smell lingered in the air when he entered. Like warm strawberry popcorn. Ben smiled to himself as Toy Co always smelled nice. It was part of the 'in-store experience' his Mum used to say. As he marvelled at the thousands of magical toys on display, the sadness slowly faded and turned to excitement. It was now *his* responsibility to make sure that Toy Co was here for years to come. To make toys that were loved and cherished by children all around the world. To maintain the legacy his Mum and Dad had left for him. As he surveyed the scene before him, it felt like baby butterflies were dancing on hot coals in his tummy. To his right was a display of cuddly toy unicorns, singing in perfect harmony. To his left, a little girl was driving an electric racing car as her parents watched with joy. He glanced up and spotted a fleet of toy rocket ships swooping and looping around a giant model solar-system that hung from the high ceiling. This place was a magical kingdom where children's imaginations could run wild. And it was a vision that his Mum and Dad had created. He was interrupted by a robot monkey that wandered over to him. "Good afternoon sir, I'm Mr Monkey. Please may I help you?" said the robot.

Ben giggled. "Good afternoon Mr Monkey, thank you for asking but I'm fine."

Mo was busy chatting to a man behind the counter, so Ben popped upstairs to the offices were his Mum and Dad used to work. He took the lift to the 8th floor, headed down the corridor and entered his Mum's old office. It was a humble place for a CEO of a £300million company. That was Ben's Mum all over; quiet, strong and understated. As much as Ben liked Penelope Weston, her office was the complete opposite! He sat down in his Mum's chair and put his feet up on the desk. A warm sensation swept through him as he stared at the wall, covered entirely with photos of Ben and his parents. The silence felt soothing. It was probably the first time in Ben's life that he'd sat in complete silence. No TV. No phone. No distraction. Just him and his thoughts. "Mum, I miss you and Dad," he said quietly. "I'm going to do you proud. I love you." He sat for a few more moments before a bolt of energy struck through him. He leapt up, kissed a photo of his Mum and Dad, and bounced out of the room. He had a spring in his step as he headed down the corridor. He now realised that the most important thing he could do in his life was to be kind and caring like his parents. To take care of Mo as she grew older, and to make sure that Toy Co continued to be one of the best toy stores in the world. As he headed towards the lift, he heard voices. He slowed down and moved towards a door that was open slightly. Ben popped his head round and saw Mike with a group of business people. They were huddled around a long table with papers and laptops sprawled out everywhere. "Uncle Mike, what's going on?" said Ben nervously.

Everyone turned around and looked at Ben with blank expressions. Mike raised his head and frowned. “Ben, what are you doing here?” he scowled. “Go on now, we have important things to discuss.”

Ben closed the door and left - the spring in his step had vanished.

Chapter Thirteen

"Right quiet down please!" ordered Mr Furrilip, donning his usual grey jumper and trousers. Ben always imagined Mr Furrilip's wardrobe at home, full to brim with grey jumpers and trousers and not a single speck of colour in sight. "Today we are going to learn about Alaska."

Ben's heart jumped in his chest. It was Monday and the previous night as he lay in bed, he had seriously considered whether to pretend to be unwell, so he wouldn't have to sit through a lesson learning about the place where his parents were eaten by a polar bear. But he decided against it as he wanted to visit Toy Co straight after school; he couldn't stop thinking about the place. So Ben gritted his teeth and sat through what was undoubtedly the longest hour of his life, even longer than an hour of rugby training. His rickety desk creaked as Ben slouched deeper into his chair. All the while a smirking Vince took great pleasure in volleying questions at a seemingly unsuspecting Mr Furrilip;

"Sir, when can we learn about the bears?"

"Sir, is it safe for humans to visit parts of Alaska?"

"Sir, what do bears eat?"

"Sir, could we possibly visit Alaska on a school trip next term?"

Vince was well and truly milking the topic to inflict maximum pain on poor Ben. Throughout, the anger in Ben grew like an unstoppable fire. Not only because Vince was making horrible comments to upset him, but he also felt a raging jealously which knotted deep inside of him. Remembering what he had heard Vince tell his friends at the weekend, why did someone like Vince Howler have a Dad and not him? Vince doesn't even like his Dad. He should be grateful he has one.

By the end of class, Ben was shaking. He jolted when the bell rang.

"Right, that's it class, see you tomorrow," shouted Mr Furrilip.

Ben was the last to leave. He waited a few minutes so Vince and his mates would be long gone. He was angry but didn't want any trouble. Besides, Vince was always with his friends and Ben would be outnumbered. He left class and headed down the corridor, pushed through the double doors, and out into the luscious grounds. The crisp autumnal air felt like a welcome relief on his warm and flustered face. His hands began to feel less shaky and his pounding heart was now beginning to relax. He watched the crowds disperse through the school gates; Vince was nowhere to be seen. He let out a deep breath and started walking towards the gates. Just as he reached halfway across the field, he heard *that voice.* "Oi Big Ben, where do you think you're going?"

It was Vince and his friends marching towards him. Ben ignored them and kept walking.

"Oi Big Ben, are you deaf? I'm talking to you," repeated Vince, this time with added venom.

With his skateboard tucked tightly under his arm, Ben didn't look back. He walked as fast as he could towards the gates, his little legs working overtime. Suddenly he felt a hand grab his rucksack and spin him round. Vince leered down at him, his white pale skin luminous in the fading light. "Listen you little wimp," he snarled. "If I talk to you, you stop and listen. You understand?" He pushed Ben sending him stumbling back. "You're such a little weed!" he laughed. "Are you sure you should be at this school? I think you need to go back to the little school."

A crowd had formed now. Ben glanced at the sea of faces surrounding them.

"What, don't you talk now?" laughed Vince. He put on a mocking baby voice as he edged closer. "Has the little orphan lost his voice now that Mummy and Daddy bear have gone?" Ben had become almost immune to the awful things Vince said to him. He stood his ground and kept his mouth shut. This made Vince even angrier. "Well, are you going to say anything baby bear?"

The crowd moved closer in, Ben started to feel claustrophobic.

"SPEAK YOU DUMBWIT!" screamed Vince, frothing at the mouth. Ben flinched at the sudden blast of nicotine breath but somehow managed to stand resolute. Finally, the school bully, the horrible and ghastly Vince Howler, moved back ever so slightly and **SLAP!** The palm of his hand connected perfectly with Ben's cherub cheek. His face stung instantly. A collective gasp and a smattering of chuckles swept the crowd. Without even thinking about it, Ben clenched his fist, levered back his right arm, and whacked Vince square on the nose. **WHACK!** Vince stumbled back as blood gushed from his nostrils and streamed into his mouth.

The crowd stepped back in shock, stunned into silence.

Ben turned and ran.

Chapter Fourteen

With his heart racing, fist throbbing, and body shaking, Ben burst through the school gates, running faster than he'd ever ran in his life. Up ahead, a crowd of boys hovered on the pavement, waiting to be picked up from school. Rows of super expensive cars were lined up alongside the side of the road, each with a smartly dressed chauffeur waiting patiently, doffing their cap as their passenger approached. "Sorry!" shouted Ben, barging his way through the throngs of people. He glanced back and spotted Vince, holding his bloody nose, chasing after him with his cronies in tow. "COME BACK YOU LITTLE…"

Ben scoured his surroundings as he wiped the sweat from his face. Everywhere he looked, the pavements were heaving with kids from school. *How could he get away from Vince and his cronies?* It was either climb over the fence and head back into school or pray that his bus turned up suddenly. Neither option was realistic, nor practical, so there was only one choice… the road. In any other situation, Ben would never use his skateboard on a busy road. His Mum and Dad, not to mention Mo, would be spitting mad at him. But desperate times called for desperate measures. With cars whizzing by, he stepped out onto the busy road and threw his skateboard to the ground. He slung his rucksack on both shoulders and inhaled a deep breath before kicking the tarmac like an angry horse. He was off! Down the hill and into town, the wind soon blowing in his hair, the sweat cooling on his face, the anxiety quickly turning to excitement. Such was the steepness of the hill, after a few seconds Ben placed both feet on the skateboard and let gravity take care of the rest. He was whizzing down the hill at an alarming pace, his tummy going crazy!

“OI! BIG BEN…”

For a split second, Ben glanced over his shoulder. At the top of the hill, he saw Vince and his friends in hot pursuit on bikes, lined up like a gang of apprentice Hell’s Angels. Behind them, it appeared the whole of the school had come to watch the action. Ben kicked hard on the road to boost his speed. His tummy was in knots as he overtook a lorry, the driver gawping through the window as this young boy on a flimsy skateboard ghosted by. Up ahead, Ben could see the traffic lights where the road split left and right. Beyond the lights was a river, the place where his Dad used to take him fishing. The trees disappeared around him as he hurtled towards the bottom of the hill. Vince and his friends had made up ground now, their heavy breathing audible as they pedalled furiously, gaining on him by the second. A huge crowd of boys from school were running down the hill, trying their best to keep up. Ben pushed against the tarmac; he was about 100 metres from the traffic lights. There was no way he could stop in time. A thousand thoughts ran through his mind as he planned his next move. The lights turned red and the cars in front began to form an orderly queue.

"THERE'S NOWHERE TO GO SKATER BOY!" screamed Vince, closing in behind him.

Ben put his foot down and kicked the road one more time with the sole of his shoe, little sparks of electricity began to fly from the wheels of his skateboard. He approached the cars in front and veered to the right. The lights were still red. Ben was heading straight for the river. In the corner of his eye, Vince suddenly came into view, now riding alongside him, his mouth and chin caked in dry blood, hissing like a maniac.

"STOP NOW YOU WET WIPE!" he screamed, aware that the river was only seconds away.

Ben smirked and carried on. Just ahead of the river was a grassy verge. Vince edged closer to Ben and with his left hand, he grabbed the boy's coat. Ben wobbled but somehow managed to keep his balance. "STOP YOU IDIOT! WHAT ARE YOU DOING?" cried Vince, visibly scared now.

They passed the traffic lights. With the rows of cars honking their horns, no doubt wondering what these two young boys were up to, Ben and Vince hit the bank of long thick grass that separated the road from the cold depths of the river. In an effort to control his bike, Vince let go of Ben. With a Nano-second to spare, Ben leaped into the grass, his skateboard tossed into the air. Vince couldn't stop, he pushed his brakes hard. And after bombing down a hill at 40mph on a bicycle, the last thing one should do is slam the brakes on.

Straight over the handlebars he flew, his long legs flapping like a freshly caught fish as he sailed through the air and landed headfirst in the river. **SPLASH!** Ben hauled himself up from the grass and watched Vince rise to the surface, the bully closely resembling a drowned rat, his face hidden from dripping wet hair. "I'M GOING TO GET YOU HAMLEY!" he screamed, paddling furiously.

Ben glanced back, and spotted Vince's friends lined up on bikes across the road. Behind them, a huge crowd of boys were just reaching the bottom of the hill on foot. Ben couldn't be completely sure, but it looked like they were all laughing hysterically. He was distracted by another wave of beeping horns from the waiting vehicles, including the lorry that Ben had overtaken just a few minutes before, the super-size vehicle's baritone horn making the car's beeps sound meek in comparison. The lights turned green and the traffic began to move. It soon blocked Ben's view of the crowd of boys over the road. Shaking from a combination of fear, adrenaline and pride, he recovered his skateboard from the long grass, and got back on the road. Ben was heading to Toy Co.

Chapter Fifteen

That was the first time in Ben's life that he'd ever punched someone. His Mum and Dad had always taught him to be kind to people, but they had made it very clear that if someone hit him first, then he must defend himself. He felt six-foot-tall as he brushed the dirt from his coat and straightened his school tie as he approached Toy Co.

The store was quiet, almost empty. He spotted Cyril hovering near the tills. "Young Ben, can I speak to you for a second?"

"Of course Cyril, how are you?"

With jet black hair, a soft Irish accent, and being only marginally taller than Ben, Cyril was the life and soul of Toy Co. Although originally employed as a security guard, over the years he had become the face of the company, his chirpy and comedic persona proving a massive hit with customers.

Cyril bounded over, his eyes watery. “Can I just say young Ben, I’m so deeply sorry to hear about your parents. They were such kind and lovely people.” His voice quivered. “Hearts of gold the pair of ‘em. I wouldn’t be here now if it wasn’t for them.”

Ben smiled. "Thank you Cyril and thank you for keeping this place safe. How are things going here?"

Cyril's face tensed up. "Well, that's what I wanted to talk to you about." He leaned closer and lowered his voice. "I don't know if I should tell you this but there were two dodgy blokes here earlier today... looking for Mike...they didn't look happy."

"Really?" asked Ben, immediately knowing who they were. "What did they look like?"

In all his years at Toy Co, Cyril had rarely experienced any trouble. As a security guard in this magical place, you could say that he had one of the most fun and stress-free jobs in the world. Although, there was one occasion, many years ago, when an elderly man on a mobility scooter accidentally knocked over a ginormous display of marbles. Within seconds, almost every inch of the floor was covered in them. That was when the poor man's scooter suddenly took on a life of its own! Used to doing speeds of 4mph, the scooter took full advantage of the sudden **impetus** from the sea of marbles. It went berserk, frenetically *zooming* around Toy Co like a **turbo-charged racing**

car with the old man clinging on for dear life! A horrified Cyril spent 20 minutes slipping and sliding about the place, desperately trying to stop the mobility scooter in its tracks. Luckily for everyone in the store that day, the scooter eventually crashed into a display of beanbags and no one was hurt. Cyril fondly refers to the experience as "*the day I lost ma' marbles*." And because this was an isolated incident in all his twenty years of service, then it was understandable that any sign of action or danger made him a little scared and indeed excited. So having Gruff and Terry visit the store was clearly something. "They were massive, built like ***wrestlers***!" he explained, eyes wide. "Big red faces. Dressed all in **black**." He shivered slightly. "They gave me the creeps." He paused then began to chuckle. "Mind you, I got covered in spit when the big one talked. Had to change ma' shirt!"

"Did Mike speak to them?" asked Ben, pretending not to know who they were.

"No, I called 'im and he told me to get rid of 'em," replied Cyril. "I don't know what he's up to, but I've never trusted the man since he stole that teddy bear." He pulled a face. "Strange man."

"Mike stole a teddy bear? When?" asked Ben incredulously.

"Didn't you know?" gossiped Cyril. "Very strange is your uncle. Very strange." He shook his head. "Anyway, that was months ago now so forget about that. You have enough on your plate laddie." He smiled and stared at the young boy for a moment. "I just wanted you to know about those two blokes Ben. Because in my eyes you're the real boss of this place."

Feeling himself redden, Ben gave an awkward smile. "Erm... thanks Cyril...that's really kind...please let me know if they come back."

"Of course boss."

Chapter Sixteen

Ben's head was swimming as he entered the lift. He knew Mike was up to no good and that Gruff and Terry had something to do with it. But what exactly where they up to? And why on earth did Mike steal a teddy bear? It didn't make sense! The lift doors opened, and Ben headed briskly down the corridor to visit his new favourite place - his Mum's office. It was starting to feel like a sanctuary, a place where Ben could relax and think. A place where he felt safe, as if somehow the photos on the wall had some kind of magical power and he could talk to his parents. He also liked sitting in the big leather chair and putting his feet up on the desk! Little did Ben know that so did someone else. He pushed the door open and entered. "Uncle Mike… Mrs Weston…what are you doing in Mum's office?" he asked sharply.

Mike hastily took his feet off the desk and sat up. "Ben? What are you doing here?"

Penelope Weston spun round in her chair and flashed that Hollywood smile. “Ah young Ben, lovely to see you. Your uncle asked me to meet him here. I’ve only just arrived. How’s school?”

“Yes Ben, shouldn’t you be at school?” asked Mike irritably.

“No, school is finished for the day,” answered Ben abruptly.

“Well run along now, I’ve got business to discuss with Mrs Weston,” said Mike.

“Call me Penelope,” smiled the lawyer, coffee in hand.

Noticing that his Mum’s old office looked different since the last time, Ben took a closer look. “Mike, why have all Mum’s photos been taken down?”

“Oh, we’re just giving the place a clean,” he replied hesitantly. “Besides, we need to look to the future.”

Ben was furious. It had been only three weeks since the funeral and Mike was already trying to erase all memories of his parents. He noticed a cardboard box of photos on the floor and angrily picked them up. “Well I’ll take these, wouldn’t want them to go missing would we?”

Without saying goodbye, Ben stormed out and walked hurriedly down the corridor, hugging the photos tightly to his chest. He couldn’t trust anyone. Uncle Mike was up to something. He could feel it. And why was Penelope there? And what was his uncle saying to all those people at the meeting yesterday? In a world of his own, he marched past the empty offices and towards the lift when he clattered into an old man mopping the floor. The man’s strong frame meant he didn’t move an inch. Ben on the other hand went flying, landing on his bum. Luckily the box of precious photos remained intact.

"Oh I'm so sorry sir," gasped Ben, picking himself up.

"That's ok young man," smiled the man. He looked at Ben for a moment. "Are you alright?"

"Yes, I'm fine thank you, I only landed on my bum," smiled the boy, brushing himself down.

The man chuckled. "No I don't mean that, I mean are *you alright*? You look like something's bothering you." He gave a warm smile and reached out a hand. "I'm Mr Mosely, I'm the caretaker around here. I'm so sorry to hear about your parents, they were such lovely and kind people. They employed me when nobody else would take me on."

"Thank you Mr Mosely," said Ben, shaking the man's calloused hand. He placed the box of photos carefully on the floor. "I'm fine I guess,' he sighed. "I just don't know who I can trust anymore."

"Young man, in life you have to trust yourself. If you feel something isn't right, then trust your instinct," said Mr Mosely, a hint of passion in his voice.

"I do feel something isn't right, but I need to do some further digging first," sighed Ben. He sat on the floor and rested his back against the wall. "How about you? How long have you been here?"

Mr Mosely placed his mop in the bucket and sat down next to Ben. His weathered face broke into a smile. "I used to be an engineer, I used to make robots in Japan," he said proudly. "I retired early so I could spend more time with my wife." He paused for a moment before saying softly, "but as luck would have it, she passed away the day I retired."

"Oh, I'm so sorry to hear that Mr Mosely," said Ben gently.

"Thank you, young man. Please, call me Tony," he said with a wry smile. "Back then, it was almost impossible to get a job in your 50's and no one would take me on. Until that is, I met your Dad."

Ben's eyes lit up. "Where did you meet him?"

"At an airport about 20 years ago," smiled Tony. "He was sat having a cup of tea trying to fix his mobile phone. They were gigantic back then, the size of a brick!" he chuckled. "I introduced myself to your Dad and fixed it for him."

"Dad was always pretty rubbish with technology," laughed Ben. "I remember when he tried to switch on the microwave with the TV remote!"

For a few moments, the pair sat in silence as Ben fiddled with the frayed cardboard box.

"It will get easier you know," said Tony gently.

"Thanks Tony. It's just..." Ben paused. "I...I still haven't cried yet." He looked at Tony. "Does that make me a bad person?"

The man gently patted Ben on the head. "It does not young man, not one little bit. People grieve in different ways." He looked at Ben, his kind green eyes watery. "You should be gentle on yourself. I bet your Mum and Dad would be extremely proud of you if they could see you now."

"Thank you," replied Ben, reddening slightly. "I just don't know who I can trust. Mum and Dad have handed over the company to me. But because I'm only eleven, my uncle is in charge until my 18th birthday." He glanced up the corridor to make sure his uncle wasn't there. He lowered his voice and leaned closer. "The thing is, I don't trust him. I've never really liked him. He's always been jealous of Dad because of his success."

"Well like you said Ben, do some further digging and if what you find gives you concern, then trust your instinct," said Tony.

Ben looked at his new friend with a glint in his eye. "Actually Tony, you may be able to help me with that."

Chapter Seventeen

That night, after having dinner with Mo, and not telling her anything about Mike, or Vince, or Gruff and Terry, or any of his worries, Ben retired to his bedroom to do his homework. He sat on his bed and flipped open his laptop. After just a few minutes, Ben couldn't concentrate. With so many thoughts running through the young boy's head, it was no surprise that he found it difficult to focus on his schoolwork. So he began to read all about his Mum and Dad's charity work. Ben was amazed, the charity his parents had founded had carried out some incredible work. They had saved endangered animals like elephants and tigers from evil deadly poachers. They had also helped prevent rainforests from being chopped down. His parents were always wildly passionate about the environment, but he'd never understood just how much work they had done. He beamed with pride and felt a steely determination to make sure their efforts didn't go to waste. He clicked on another page and noticed some work his parents had done in Alaska. So that must be why they were there? Toy Co Foundation had donated £2million to a charity in Alaska to prevent a decline in polar bears. Ben slammed his laptop shut and felt a pang of anger. He lay in his bed and stared at the ceiling. So Mum and Dad tried to save the polar bears and in return they kill them? Life isn't fair.

*** CEO ***

"Morning poppet, did you sleep well?" asked Mo, humming to herself as she pottered in the kitchen.

Ben rubbed his eyes. "Not really Mo, I was tossing and turning all night." He slumped at the breakfast bar and sighed. "The world is such a cruel place."

Mo poured him a glass of orange. "Oh my darling, whatever do you mean?"

"I was looking at Mum and Dad's charity work last night," he sighed before taking a gulp of fresh orange juice. "They donated £2million to save the polar bears and in the end, the polar bears killed them!" He tossed a butter knife which clattered on the table.

"Oh my dear, you know sometimes the world isn't fair," she said in her soft Scottish brogue. "But your Mum and Dad died doing something they loved. Something they were passionate about." She stood behind Ben, placing her hands on his shoulders. "Although they aren't physically here anymore, they are still here in spirit." Tears started to form in her eyes. "Look around you. Look at the legacy they've left behind. Toy Co, this house, all of the fantastic charities they've supported." She paused for a moment. "And best of all, they've left it all to you to take over."

"But what happens if I'm not good enough?" asked Ben, his voice shaky. "What happens if when I turn 18, I'm not able to run the company and do all of the amazing things they've done."

Tears streamed down Mo's plump cheeks. "You will Ben, I know it."

Chapter Eighteen

That afternoon, Ben walked into class with a lingering sense of paranoia lurking at the back of his mind. Since yesterday's escapades in which he had punched Vince Howler in the nose, before leading him a merry dance down the hill and into the river, the horrible bully hadn't said a word to him. This was highly unusual, and it made Ben deeply suspicious. He hoped Vince's silence was due to fact that Ben had stood up for himself, but he knew better than that. He knew Vince wouldn't stop picking on him that easily.

"Hi Ben," said Vince cheerfully, sat at his usual desk. His nose was swollen, the colour of a bruised apple. "How are you today?"

Vince was definitely up to something. Ben walked by and ignored him. He dumped his bag on the floor and sat in his usual spot, right at the back of the class where he could see everyone, and no one could see him.

"Ben, could you come over here a second?" asked Vince. "I've got something for you."

The class fell silent, all eyes on Ben. "What is it Vince?" he sighed, exasperated.

"Come here and I'll show you," replied Vince, being uncharacteristically polite.

"No thanks, I'll get whatever it is after class," said Ben, getting his workbook out of his bag.

Mr Furrilip intervened. "Benjamin, we're starting class in a second, why don't you take Vince up on his kind offer so we can all get started?"

"But sir, surely it would make sense to start class now and I'll speak to Vince afterwards?" asked Ben incredulously.

"Just get on with it Benjamin," sighed Mr Furrilip, his bony hands on his skinny hips.

Wearing the expression of an angel, Vince's usual rat-features were now almost mouse-like. If you didn't know the real Vince, and you had never met him before, you could be fooled into thinking he was a rather sweet boy. Ben knew it was all an act and that the bully had an ulterior motive. But with pressure from

Mr Furrilip to see what Vince wanted, Ben let out a dramatic sigh and went to stand up. “What the…” he mumbled. Trying to force the chair from his bum, but failing miserably, Ben discovered that he was in fact stuck to it! Like a dog chasing his tail, the young boy spun round in a circle and the chair duly followed.

"What are you doing Benjamin?" barked Mr Furrilip.

"Sir, the chair is stuck to my trousers," cried Ben, his face bright red.

The class burst into hysterics. Vince Howler and his cronies almost fell from their chairs with laughter - *at least they had the option of falling from their chairs.*

Even Mr Furrilip looked like he was trying his best to remain serious. "Benjamin Hamley, please get out. You have disrupted this class yet again."

"But sir, why would I do this on purpose?" asked Ben. He looked at Vince. "He did this!"

"Nonsense," spat Mr Furrilip. "You have a history of playing jokes."

"Not on myself!" cried Ben.

Mr Furrilip nodded to the door. "Out of this classroom **NOW**!"

Ben huffed and bent down to collect his bag. In case you've ever wondered, bending down with a chair stuck to your bottom is rather difficult. "Sir, I can't reach my bag," he said meekly.

His classmates burst into laughter again.

There was lots of grunting and groaning as Mr Furrilip marched up to Ben, picked up his bag and slung it at the young boy. “Straight to the Cruncher’s office...erm...I mean Miss Cruncher’s office now!”

Chapter Nineteen

With the chair stuck firmly to his bum, Ben caught a glimpse of his reflection in the window and couldn't help but chuckle. Admittedly, he admired the comic value of pulling such a prank. Though his smile was only fleeting, as he knew that coming from Vince Howler, comedy wasn't the main intention. Ben followed Mr Furrilip's orders and made his way towards the door. This was when he discovered that walking was also a challenge with a chair glued to your rear. In full view of his classmates, he waddled like a duck making slow progress down the aisle of desks. Cue another round of insatiable laughter and cruel jibes. Sweat pouring from his face, he eventually reached the door and without turning back, slammed it shut behind him. In the stillness and quietness of the corridor, Ben breathed a sigh of relief as his face cooled. He plonked himself down in the chair and laughed - there was an upside to having a chair permanently stuck to his bum – at least he always had a seat! Ben couldn't face seeing

Miss Cruncher. The terrible woman's misty breath was the last thing he needed. She would only go ballistic and besides, Ben really didn't care anymore. He was fed up of school and had had enough of the wretched place. He thought about Toy Co and the butterflies in his belly returned. Ben suddenly remembered that he had a spare pair of trousers in his bag, Mo had always made him take a spare pair to school just in case they got dirty or ripped. He'd always thought it was pointless carrying them around with him. But now they were just what he needed (Mo was *always right).* Alone in the corridor, he skilfully freed himself from the chair by squeezing out of his trousers. Now wearing just his shirt, socks and pants but no chair, Ben suddenly felt free. "Ah that's better!" he cried, enjoying the sensation of standing up straight. He hurriedly put the spare trousers on and grabbed his bag. He was just about to leave when he glanced at the chair with the empty trouser legs hanging limply from it. Ben chuckled; it looked as if he'd vanished into thin air! To his right, was Mr Bones' classroom. An enormously muscly teacher who taught Biology. He poked his head into the empty classroom and spotted a human skeleton hanging from a frame. Trying to stop himself from giggling too loudly, he carried the skeleton from class before carefully slipping its legs into his old trousers. Holding his breath to prevent him from bursting into laughter, Ben manoeuvred the legs so one was crossed over the other. With the skeleton's tall gangly frame sitting upright in the chair, and Ben's trousers being way too short for its long legs, the skeleton bore a canny resemblance to Mr Furrilip!

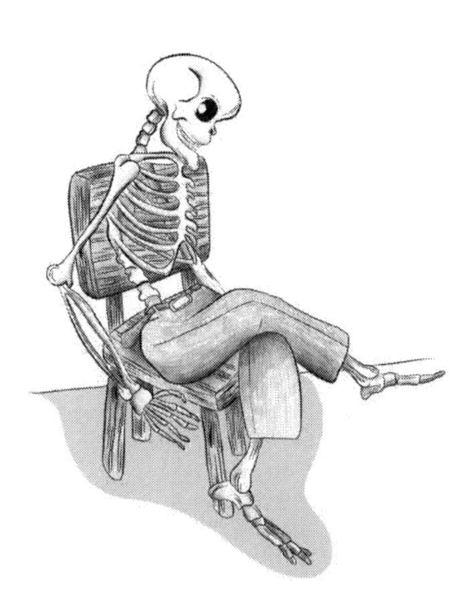

Feeling proud of his creation and tempted to wait and see the reaction of Mr Furrilip and his classmates, Ben had to go; he had more important things to do. He grabbed his bag and skipped down the corridor. It was time to head to Toy Co to find out what his uncle is up to.

Chapter Twenty

Turning onto the blustery high street, the autumn leaves blowing everywhere, Ben skilfully navigated his skateboard through the crowds of shoppers when he spotted blue flashing lights up ahead. Eager to see what was going on, he flicked his foot to the ground and quickly built up speed; he swerved past a busker before almost colliding with a street artist posing as a statue. Toy Co suddenly came into view, and as he drew nearer, he noticed a small crowd and a police car outside. Then he spotted Cyril, pacing up and down, wearing a worried look. Ben stepped off his skateboard and ran over. "Cyril... Cyril...what's going on? What's happened?"

Visibly shaking, Cyril spoke a million miles an hour. "Oh Ben, it was two people on a motorbike, rode up to the front entrance, smashed the window with a hammer and sped off." He leaned against the wall. "No one was hurt though." He sighed. "It all happened so fast."

Relieved no one was hurt, but immediately feeling suspicious, Ben asked, “where’s Mike?”

Cyril nodded inside. “In there talking to the police. Do you think…”

“I think I know what you’re thinking Cyril,” said Ben, cutting him off mid-sentence.

“Let’s keep that to ourselves for now. I need to speak to Mike.”

*** CEO ***

“Ah Ben, what a surprise,” sighed Mike, reclining in his chair. In Ben’s *Mum’s old chair*. Looking a bit too comfortable for Ben’s liking.

Entering the office, Ben felt warm suddenly. “What’s going on Mike? Who smashed the window?”

“Calm down Ben, it was nothing,” he smirked. “I spoke to the police; it was just kids.” He leaned forward and gave an unpleasant look that Ben had never seen before. “It was probably those dirty homeless people,” he scowled. “I’ll call the council tomorrow and get them moved on.”

Now starting to see what his uncle was really like, Ben was angry. "Those people on the streets need our help. And we will help them!" he cried. "Cyril told me that two men turned up yesterday. They sounded like Gruff and Terry."

Mike flinched slightly before regaining his composure. "Oh Cyril is talking nonsense," he spat. "All that man does is gossip! They were just delivery drivers questioning an order." He sighed. "Look Ben, I know you want to help but please leave running this company to me. This isn't school. This is business. And you are just a child."

Ben wasn't deterred, he pressed firmly, "well why did you steal a teddy bear then?"

His face tightened for a moment. "Let me guess...Cyril the squirrel told you? Now why would I steal a teddy bear?

Ben could read his uncle like a book; he knew he was trying to fob him off. "What are you up to Mike? Who are those men?"

Slamming his fist on the desk suddenly, Mike leaned forward and growled, "look Ben, I really don't have time for this. I’ve got a company to run. Haven’t you got homework to do? Go now. I’ll see you later.”

Ben turned and left.

Chapter Twenty One

Furious with his uncle, Ben stormed out of his Mum's old office and went to find Tony. Yesterday he had asked the old man to act as his spy. His mission was simple; to find out what Mike is up to. You see, unfortunately in this world, a lot of people are too 'busy' or full of self-importance to acknowledge a person who carries out important duties such as a caretaker or a cleaner. They think such a job is below them. They fail to see and appreciate the tireless work that goes on around them in keeping their place of work clean and safe. So who better than Tony to go undercover and eavesdrop on Mike's conversations? Although Ben wasn't aware of this unfortunate aspect of grown-up life, it was this very reason why he had unwittingly come up with a genius plan. He continued down the corridor until he spotted the old man in an empty office fixing a computer. "Hello Tony, how are you doing?" said Ben, poking his head through the doorway.

Tony put his screwdriver down and smiled. “Oh hi young man. How are you?” He took a seat and sighed. “Have you seen the window downstairs? I’ve just finished sweeping all of the glass outside. I heard it was kids. A real shame but what can you do? I’ve ordered a new window anyhow.”

There and then, Ben quickly decided not to tell Tony about Gruff and Terry. He didn’t want him involved in any of that. There was a long moment of silence as Ben sat down. “What is it Tony? You don’t know anything about the window do you?”

Tony spread his large hands flat on the desk and gave a heavy sigh. “It’s nothing to do with the window. It’s worse than that...earlier today, I listened in on a meeting with Mike and the board of directors.” He shifted in his seat. “It’s not good news I’m afraid Ben. Toy Co is in trouble. Big trouble.” He sighed. “The company isn’t making any money and by the sounds of it, it could close down after Christmas.”

“What? But how?” cried Ben, his face heating up suddenly. “I thought Toy Co was one of the biggest toy stores in the world?”

"You're right Ben, Toy Co *was* one of the biggest toy stores. But not anymore," sighed Tony.

"This would never have happened if Mum and Dad were still here," said Ben angrily. He paused for a moment. "Why is Mike in charge? I can't believe Mum and Dad let him run the company last year, it doesn't make sense."

"I'm sorry Ben, I can't tell you that," said Tony. "This little old caretaker isn't privy to such information."

"Do you think Mike is destroying Toy Co on purpose?" asked Ben.

"No I don't think he's that clever," said Tony with a wry smile. "I think he's just out of his depth." He leaned forward. "It was pretty clear that he doesn't have a clue what he's talking about. The directors were asking him lots of questions and he couldn't answer any of them."

Ben felt powerless. His Mum and Dad's company was in trouble and he needed to save it. But how? For a start he needed to learn what these funny words meant like ‘director’ and ‘board’. “Tony, who are the directors and what do they do?” he asked.

Tony stood up and smiled. “Well young man, seeing as you are technically the owner of this place, you should really know how it all works.”

Ben made himself comfortable and watched intently as Tony approached a whiteboard and began drawing a diagram.

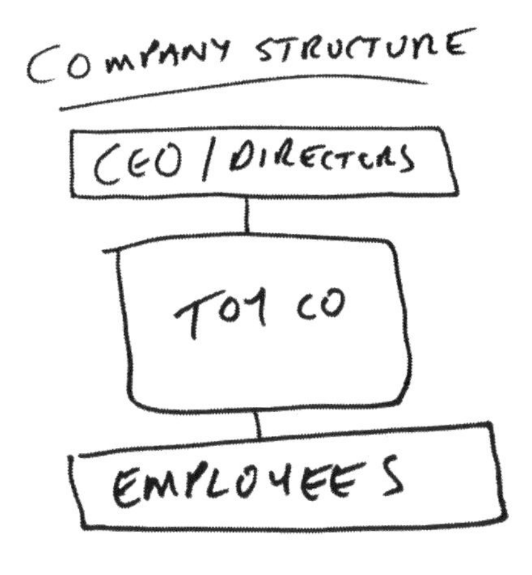

“The directors have invested money in Toy Co. This means that they own part of the company,” explained Tony.

"So Mum and Dad didn't own all of it?"

"No but they did own most of it," he answered. "And now you do." He thought for a moment and smiled. "Let's just pretend that Toy Co is a pizza...." Ben felt his tummy rumble suddenly as Tony went on, "...now imagine that you make this pizza yourself. You go to the shops, you buy the ingredients, then you go home and make the pizza by hand."

"Sounds like a lot of hard work to me," chuckled Ben. "I could order one and have it delivered in 30 minutes!"

"Ah yes you could young man," smiled Tony. "But what would be the fun in that?" He moved away from the whiteboard and sat down to face the young boy. "Now let's just say that the ingredients for the pizza cost you £5 and after you made the dough and sprinkled over the ingredients you pop it in the oven." Tony paused for a moment. "Then when you take the pizza out of the oven, it not only smells delicious but it's enormous! In fact, it's the biggest pizza in the world with eight gigantic slices, each the size of a surfboard!"

"Wow £5 is a bargain for the biggest pizza in the world!" smiled Ben, his mouth watering.

Tony was in his element, his eyes lighting up. "It is indeed. But it would be even more of a bargain if you ate only four slices..."

"That would never happen! I love pizza too much" laughed Ben. He pulled a face. "But how would it be even more of a bargain if I didn't eat it all?"

"Aha" winked Tony, standing up and returning to the whiteboard. "So let's just say that you had four slices leftover and all of a sudden, four people approached you and offered to buy a slice each for £1"

Ben worked the numbers out in his head. "Wow that's a good deal, I'd take £4. I could almost make another pizza then!"

"Exactly," said Tony passionately. "You got it in one! Your Mum and Dad made their own pizza and called it Toy Co." He drew a pizza on the whiteboard. "And the company turned out to be like this pizza, beautiful and gigantic. So beautiful that other people wanted a slice." He smiled. "So your parents sold a few slices to other people who then became directors. Then your parents used that money to make the pizza even bigger and more delicious."

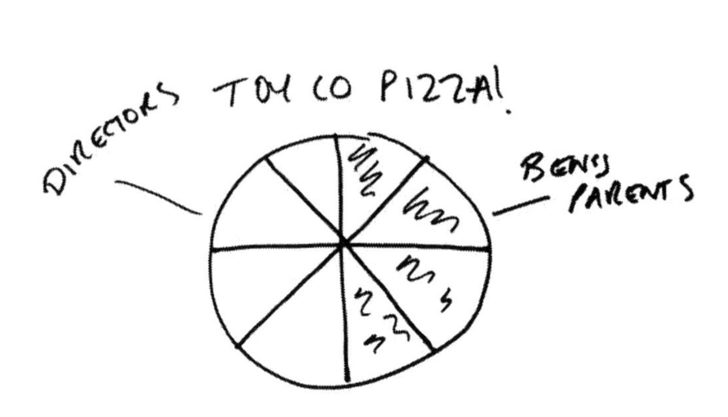

Ben nodded enthusiastically as he began to understand what Tony was saying. "So the directors own part of the pizza...erm...I mean Toy Co. Does that mean they get to choose the ingredients?"

"You are such a clever young boy you know that Ben?" grinned Tony, beaming with pride. "They do indeed. Only the ingredients in the case of Toy Co aren't things like cheese and pepperoni. They are the toys that Toy Co sells, and the people it employs, or the way it promotes the company."

"So the directors have a say in all of that?" asked Ben, hanging on his every word. "What happens if they want to leave?"

"They would have to sell their slice," smiled Tony. "In business terms we call them 'shares'."

Tony was such a great teacher. Much better than Mr Furrilip, although that was hardly the greatest of compliments. The only similarity Ben could think of was the time when Mr Furrilip had leftover pizza crust stuck in his terrible moustache. "I know Mum was the CEO but what did my Dad do at Toy Co?" he asked.

"Ah, your Dad was the Chairman," said Tony, a twinkle in his eye. He approached the whiteboard again and drew a block on the diagram to represent the Chairman. "The CEO runs the company and the Chairman runs the board of directors."

Ben jumped up and began pacing the office, chewing a pen in his mouth. Tony chuckled at how grown up the young boy looked. "So Tony, what can we do to save Toy Co?"

"Simple. A really strong Christmas," replied the man. "Toy Co needs a best-selling toy before Christmas."

"But that is less than three months away," worried Ben.

Chapter Twenty Two

It was pouring down by the time Ben got home. He walked through the door soaked to the bone. What a day it had been! Even though his parents were super rich, he had lived a pretty normal life up until now. But in the last three weeks, he'd had enough adventures to last a lifetime. He was greeted by a smiling Mo and the mouth-watering aroma of spaghetti Bolognese and garlic bread. Ben was slowly getting used to coming home and having only Mo for company. In this huge house it did feel rather empty at times, but Mo's super-sized heart and kindness helped fill most of the void.

After a quick shower, Ben joined Mo at the table. The dining room was cosy, with the roaring open fire, the curtains drawn, and the wind and rain battering against the windows. He had decided not to tell Mo about Vince, nor his suspicions about Mike, but he did want to find out why his awful uncle was put in charge of Toy Co. So he casually mentioned that he'd heard the company was experiencing difficult times. "Mo, do you know why Mike was put in charge of Toy Co last year?" he asked while twirling spaghetti around his fork.

Mo put her knife and fork down and sighed. "Well…your uncle had been moaning to your Dad for a long time. He wanted something to do after he split up with his last girlfriend."

"Daphne?" asked Ben.

"No not Daphne, the other one, what was her name?" pondered Mo.

"Frankie?"

"No he was with Frankie years ago."

"Barbara?" asked Ben.

"Which one was Barbara?" asked Mo.

"The bald one who rode a motorbike," replied Ben.

"No not her."

"Sophie?"

"Which one was Sophie?" asked Mo.

"The one who always wore odd socks."

"No it wasn't her."

"Doris?"

"Which one was Doris?"

"The one who disappeared one day and never came back," answered Ben.

Mo laughed. "Mike has had more girlfriends than I've had hot puddings!" She tore off a piece of garlic bread. "Anyway, whichever girlfriend he was with last year, when they split up, he felt lost and asked your Dad for more responsibility at Toy Co."

"And Dad just said yes?"

"Not exactly," smiled Mo. "It took a couple of months before your Mum and Dad agreed. They never trusted Mike you see. But eventually they came round."

"What made them change their mind?"

"You," smiled Mo. "Your Mum and Dad wanted to spend more time with you, so they let Mike run the company for a while."

"Oh," said Ben. A wave of guilt swept over him as he swallowed a mouthful of spaghetti. "So Toy Co is in this mess because of me?"

"No my dear," said Mo fiercely. "Absolutely not. It's in this mess because of your stupid uncle. You need to stop blaming yourself my precious. None of this is your fault."

"I still haven't cried yet," said Ben, playing with his food. "I feel so guilty. I keep thinking Mum and Dad are disappointed in me because I haven't cried."

Mo leaned over the table and tilted the young boy's chin, so he faced her head on. "Look Ben, none of this is your fault. The way you're coping with all of this is amazing. People show their emotions in different ways. You don't have to cry. Now come here and give your Auntie Mo a big cuddle." She got up and walked round the table to him. Ben smiled as Mo hugged him. "You know poppet, sometimes in life there is nothing better than a cuddle," she whispered.

"Thanks Mo," said Ben. "I think you've just gave me an idea."

*** CEO ***

Ben's brain was buzzing with ideas as he kissed Mo goodnight and ran upstairs to his bedroom. What does every child like more than anything? A cuddle! A big hug that's what! Ben hopped onto his bed and flipped open the laptop. He stared at the screen and browsed through the photos of the magnificent animals that the Toy Co Foundation had saved. He flicked through the photos excitedly before stopping at a picture of a majestic polar bear, its white furry coat glistening in the Arctic sun.

Ben had a lightbulb moment - he knew what he had to do to save Toy Co.

Chapter Twenty Three

It was a glorious sunny morning as Tony entered Toy Co. “Morning Cyril!” he chirped, waving to the security guard.

Toy Co was Tony’s life. When his wife passed away many years ago, it came as a terrible shock. And with his children and grandchildren living in Australia, and only his pet dog Dixie to keep him company, Tony suddenly found himself alone. It was at the airport ahead of a long flight to visit his children when he met Ben’s Dad. At that point, Tony was figuring out what to do with the rest of his life. His children wanted him to move to Australia, but Tony loved his home and he wanted to stay there. It was that chance encounter with Mr Hamley that gave Tony a new lease of life. He was given a job and from the minute he returned from Australia, he joined Ben’s parents and threw everything into making Toy Co a success. The last twenty years had been an incredible experience, helping to build the very first store, a modest toy shop down a side street, to now maintaining the world famous flagship store in the most prestigious part of town. A store that hundreds of thousands of tourists flocked to from all over the world each year. He would do everything he could to help Ben save this place.

Whistling cheerfully as he entered the lift, Tony checked his watch, it was 9am on the dot. His mood was quickly dampened when the lift doors opened and there stood Mike, with a face like thunder. "Tom, what time do you call this?" he huffed, his face flustered. "Come on, I've got an important presentation to give to the directors. The projector screen isn't working. I need you to fix it."

It didn't bother Tony that Mike had always called him 'Tom'. Although he could never work out whether Mike did it on purpose or if he was just very bad at remembering names. Sadly, Tony had a hunch that it was the former, as he always wore a name badge which clearly stated his name. Despite having to put up with such awful behaviour, Tony was always kind and polite to Mike. Not because he liked him, or because he was his boss, but the old man was a firm believer that you should always be kind to others as you never know what problems people may have.

"Ok Mike, sorry I wasn't aware of the meeting. I'll fix the projector now," he replied cheerily.

Tony walked briskly to the meeting room and entered. Lamps hung low from the ceiling, offering a dim glow over the long boardroom table where the directors were sat. Wearing smart business attire, they busily typed away at laptops, stopping only for an occasional slurp of coffee; they didn't even acknowledge Tony when he entered (*see, I told you so*). Nevertheless, he smiled politely and clambered under the table to check the projector cables. After a few moments he popped his head out. The projector screen flickered into life and Mike's presentation was displayed on the big screen.

"What was wrong with it?" asked Mike abruptly.

Tony returned to a standing position. "I just switched it off and turned it back on again."

The directors chuckled.

Mike blushed. "Ah, well ok then," he replied. "Thank you Tom, I think we're having issues with the laptop so please stay here while I deliver this presentation. Just in case anything else breaks."

"Of course Mike," replied Tony. He made his way to the corner of the room and sat down to watch Mike deliver his presentation.

Chapter Twenty Four

Positioned at the head of the table, in a garish red velvet suit, Mike cleared his throat. “Ahem...good morning everyone, so we’ll get straight down to business. As you know we are in difficult times. You have the agenda in front of you to discuss two very important items.”

Toy Co: URGENT board meeting
Attendees: Mike Hamley, Mrs Chopra, Mr Owen, and Mr Howler

Agenda

1. Proposal for Christmas Flagship Toy
2. Proposal for sale of Toy Co
3. AOB

Mike took a seat. “So we all agree that we need a miraculous Christmas to save the company. And to do that, I would like to present to you a very special toy. A toy which I think will be a best seller.” Mike stood up, his face beaming with excitement. “This is the toy to save Toy Co and make us rich!” he cried. Mike quickly backtracked, “err...I mean enrich the lives of children across the world." He flicked the presentation slides on the screen. "Ladies and gentlemen, I would like to present to you... **'Filbert Franstein!'"**

On the projector screen, an image appeared of Filbert Franstein, Mike's new creation.

This was evidently his idea for a toy that would sell millions and save Toy Co from ruin. And no doubt put Mike's name up in lights. Tony watched with intrigue from the dark corner of the boardroom and chuckled quietly under his breath. The toy looked dreadful; its skinny lime green body was reminiscent of a streak of elastic snot; the kind of snot you only get when you feel *really* unwell. Presumably based on Mary Shelley's classic book '*Frankenstein*', in which a scientist creates a fearsome monster, Filbert looked anything but scary. He looked more like a cross between a meerkat and an alien on a diet. Tony chuckled to himself as he studied the image on screen; with its tiny **black** eyes, *long* **pointy** nose and *sloped* chin, Filbert bore an uncanny resemblance to his creator! The directors didn't say a word as Mike paced the room, his eyes wandering around the table, eager to gauge any kind of reaction. The deathly silence was interrupted by a bald man taking an enthusiastic slurp of coffee.

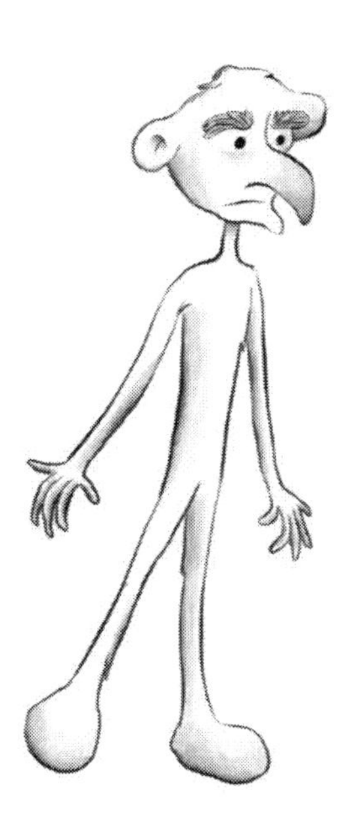

"Well," said Mike, rapping his fingers on the table. "Thoughts?"

A few more moments of silence passed before the bald man spoke. He removed his glasses. "Mike, I appreciate the effort you've put into this...erm...

thing...but to be quite frank, it looks terrible and no child or parent is going to want to buy that."

Mike's face turned puce. "Thank you Mr Howler, maybe you need more time to think about it?"

"I'm sorry Mike, but it's a disaster. I don't need any more time to think about it," replied the man. He took another gulp of coffee. "In fact, if I had more time to think about it I'd probably say something much worse!"

The other directors laughed.

A bead of sweat trickled down Mike's neck. "Anyone else?"

"I agree with Mr Howler," said an Indian lady. "To put it bluntly Mike, it looks like an old wet rag." She closed her notebook. "Without wanting to be rude, I wouldn't clean the toilet with it." She smiled. "In fact, I wouldn't let my cleaner clean the toilet with it!"

Another smattering of chuckles swept the room.

Mike loosened his tie and slumped in his chair. The dim lights beamed onto his lunar forehead like a beacon. “Well,” he sighed. “Unless anyone disagrees with Mr Howler and Mrs Chopra, I guess we should move onto item two; the potential sale of Toy Co.”

Tony looked on, he almost felt sorry for Mike...well almost. He watched as the hapless man pressed a button on the laptop and the projector screen went blank. “Stupid thing!” he cried, before jabbing the keyboard with his finger. “Tom, will you come and fix this?” he asked impatiently.

Tony stood up and approached the table. He leaned over and fiddled with the wires, pressed a few buttons, and like magic, the screen switched back on.

“Thanks Tom,” huffed Mike.

Tony merely nodded. Leaning up from the table, he accidently knocked Mike’s coffee and it spilled over a huge pile of papers.

"What have you done, you stupid buffoon!" boomed Mike.

"I'm sorry sir," blushed Tony. "It was an accident."

"I don't care if it was an accident, you've ruined my papers," said Mike crossly. "Please just get out will you."

Tony trudged towards the door. The eyes of the board members followed his journey, their faces expressionless. The room was silent. The atmosphere strained. Tony subtly smiled to himself as he closed the door behind him, Mike was clearly under pressure.

"Sorry about that ladies and gentlemen," said Mike, regaining his composure. "Now, let's discuss item two. We've received an offer from 'Toy Universe' to buy Toy Co."

Chapter Twenty Five

"Why would we sell Toy Co?" asked a man with a bushy beard.

"And to a competitor!" wailed Mr Howler.

Mike stood up and rubbed his face. "You see Mr Owen, as you know we are in financial trouble. Serious trouble. Toy Universe have offered £300million to buy the whole company." He couldn't hide his delight. "Think about it everyone, £300million."

There were inaudible mutterings around the boardroom table. Mr Owen, a director with bright red hair and a dull grey beard, spoke up, "so why have you just tried to suggest a new toy for Christmas? If you wanted to sell the company, why would you go to all that effort to design a toy!" Mr Owen glanced around the room. "From my perspective Mike, it seems like you don't have a clue what you're doing!"

There were murmurs of approval around the table. Mike had clearly lost the confidence of the directors. He sat down and took a sip of water. “Mr Owen, thank you for your comments. Please let me explain.” He shuffled his papers. “You see, my suggestion for a toy was to illustrate the fact that we are simply behind the times.” He stood up and began pacing the room. “Our creative teams are lagging behind. We have run out of steam. We have no ideas. The other toy companies are racing ahead, creating dynamic and exciting toys that are selling by the bucket load.” A smile appeared on Mike’s face, he was getting into a groove now. “We are a relic of the past, of a time when a cuddly toy was enough for a child. Now children want robots. They want toys that talk and jump and dance. We just don't have that capability."

"But we do!" argued Mr Owen. "I was greeted by a robot monkey when I walked in!"

"Ah but you see, that monkey is just a prototype. We don't have the capability of making them in thousands," smiled Mike, he was growing in confidence now.

"So why don't we invest in new people? Why don't we hire some of the creative talent we clearly need?" asked Mrs Chopra.

"Because Mrs Chopra, we don't have the money to do that. Unless, we fire half of our staff," replied Mike.

"I think we need some time to think about this," said Mr Howler, his hands clasped together. "This is a huge decision and I think we'd like to discuss it in private before we resume."

"Of course," smiled Mike.

"Please may I ask, why are you so interested in selling the company? You don't own any of it do you?" asked Mrs Chopra.

Mike's expression turned sour. "No Mrs Chopra I do not. However, I owe it to my late brother and sister-in-law to preserve the legacy and reputation of Toy Co. If that means selling it then so be it."

"But you'll be out of a job then," said Mr Owen. "What are you going to do?"

"I'll find something I'm sure," smirked Mike.

Chapter Twenty Six

Ben burst out of the school gates, kicked his skateboard to the ground and set off down the hill. Despite his parents being super rich, they had always insisted that Ben travel by bus to school. They wanted him to understand the real world and live a 'normal' life. It would have been much easier for Ben to have a limousine pick him up like all the other boys. But Ben loved hopping on the bus, especially when Barbara, his favourite bus driver was on duty. She had a soft spot for Ben and he always sat at the front to chat to her when the bus was stuck in traffic. But since Vince had chased him down the hill a few days ago, Ben had come to realise that he was pretty good on a skateboard. It was also amazing fun to travel at such speed – to hear the sound of the wheels burning like fire on the concrete – the vibrations that ran through his body when he went over the tiniest of bumps - the low sense of gravity - skateboarding was simply awesome. It made him feel free and powerful. And anyway, it was much faster than going by bus. As he reached the high street and approached Toy Co, he spotted a homeless girl slouched in a shop doorway a few doors down. Ben stepped off his skateboard and approached her. “Excuse me, are you ok?”

“Me?” asked the girl. She swept her matted hair away to reveal a gaunt but pretty face with a button nose and warm eyes like mini-chocolate brownies.

Ben sat cross-legged on the pavement and faced the girl. "Hi I'm Ben. I just wondered if you were ok?"

Tears formed in her eyes, there was a long moment of silence before she cleared her throat and said, "oh…thank you…nice to meet you Ben… I'm Hannah." She eyed him suspiciously. "Why are you talking to me? Nobody ever talks to me."

"Oh," said Ben. He paused for a moment, he felt embarrassed suddenly. "Erm…because I wanted to see if you were ok."

"Oh," said the girl.

The pair laughed nervously.

"Can I get you something to eat or put you up for the night somewhere?" asked Ben.

Hannah was taken aback. "I don't know what to say…why…that…that...would be amazing," she said softly. She raised her head before wrapping a manky blanket over her shoulders "It's getting cold now…seeing the Christmas lights in the shop windows makes me feel colder…and lonelier."

Ben immediately felt for Hannah. She looked young, probably only a few years older than him. He didn't want to ask her too many questions, so he said, "well you just wait here. I'll be back very soon. Lovely to meet you Hannah, I'll be back!"

Chapter Twenty Seven

"Good afternoon Cyril," whistled Ben as he strode through the doors. He noticed that it was quiet again in Toy Co, he could see only one customer; a little old lady trying out a remote control car.

"Afternoon boss!" replied Cyril cheerfully.

"Can I speak to you for a second?" asked Ben.

"Of course young man," smiled Cyril, his emerald eyes lighting up.

Ben moved closer and spoke quietly, "I wondered if you could do me a favour," he said. "There's a girl outside, her name is Hannah and she's homeless. I would like her to sleep in the shop at night. Do we have security guards in overnight?"

"I'm afraid we don't young man, we all finish at 7pm," explained Cyril.

"Oh," said Ben, slightly disappointed. "Well, do you think people would want to work night shifts?"

Cyril thought for a moment. "Well I'm sure everyone could do with the extra cash with Christmas coming up."

"Brilliant," said Ben, his excitement returning. "Because I've noticed at least 15 homeless people outside these last few days. And I want us to provide a place for them to sleep until they find themselves a home. Can you speak to your team and see what they think?"

"Yes boss, we'd need at least two or three people on shift if we have 15 people to look after," explained Cyril.

Ben smiled. "That doesn't matter. We'll also pay double for night shifts. Please can you speak to your team and come back to me with a plan?"

"Yes boss, do you think we should involve a homeless charity just to get some advice?" asked Cyril.

"Yes good idea! Please let Hannah in tonight and then by tomorrow it would be brilliant to let the others stay here as well."

Cyril chuckled. "You know Ben, you're wise beyond your years you are. Just like your Mum and Dad."

"Thanks Cyril," he said bashfully, reddening slightly as he headed towards the lift.

He reached the lift doors and turned suddenly. "Cyril," he called.

"Yes young man?"

"Don't tell Mike."

Chapter Twenty Eight

Ben was elated as the lift took him to the 8th floor. He studied himself in the mirror, he felt older – wiser even. The young boy now had a purpose - to save Toy Co and to help other people. He had so much money and he simply didn't need it. All he needed was his skateboard and a roof over his head. As long as Mo was ok that was the main thing. Despite losing his parents, Ben had come to realise that he was extremely lucky to still have a home to return to each night. The lift doors opened; the corridor quiet. "Tony, are you still around?" he called. No answer. He headed down the corridor and spotted a man mopping the floor. "Oh hello there, I'm looking for Mr Moseley," said Ben.

The man turned round, he was much younger than Tony. "Oh hi there," he replied. "I'm Phil, I just started today."

"Hi Phil, welcome to Toy Co!" replied Ben enthusiastically. "I don't suppose you've seen Mr Moseley have you?"

Phil thought for a moment. "Mr Moseley doesn't ring a bell I'm afraid. What was his first name?

"Tony."

Phil rested his mop in the bucket. "Ah yes Tony! I haven't met him, but he is the bloke who left today. Stormed out apparently. That's why I'm here." He chuckled. "I'm the new Tony!"

"**What**?" wailed Ben incredulously, his heart racing. "Tony left? But he loved this place!" He sat on an old desk to think for a moment, his legs swinging backwards and forwards.

"Yes, well apparently he was rude and violent when he left. Threatened to hit Mike and tell lots of lies about the company" gossiped Phil.

"But that doesn't sound like Tony," said Ben. "I need to find him." He shuffled his bum from the desk and stood up. "It was a pleasure to meet you Phil and thank you for joining us, I'll see you soon."

As Ben headed down the corridor, Phil called out. "Excuse me, sorry I didn't catch your name."

The young boy turned and smiled. "I'm Ben Hamley, CEO of Toy Co."

Chapter Twenty Nine

How could Mike fire Tony? Ben was certain that his uncle was up to no good. He felt really sorry for Tony, and although sadness hung in the depths of his tummy, Ben couldn't help but chuckle at the irony; ten minutes ago he was going up in the lift and felt on top of the world; now he was heading down in the lift and he felt low. Maybe they should invent lifts that only go up?

The lift doors opened, and Ben walked briskly through the store and towards the exit. He was just about to leave when Cyril came rushing over, his face beaming with excitement. "Hello boss, before you go, I've spoken to the team, everyone is up for doing night shifts. I've worked out a system and everything!"

"Sorry Cyril, I don't know what you mean," replied Ben solemnly.

Taken aback, Cyril's smile disappeared. "Are you ok young man? I was talking about helping the homeless people. You know, giving them somewhere to sleep? We were talking about it ten minutes ago."

"Oh yes oh that. I'm sorry Cyril. It's just that Tony has been fired," he sighed.

"I know Ben I heard," said Cyril. He lowered his voice. "No one is safe round here. Look, if you don't want us to go ahead with the homeless shelter we can leave it for now if you want?"

Ben's mood lifted. "No Cyril, let's do it. Thank you so much for arranging it so quickly!"

Cyril smiled. "Thanks young man, I've also spoken to the local homeless charity. They are going to come down for the first few nights."

"Amazing Cyril, thank you so much!"

Cyril's excitement returned. "When we close the store at 5pm, that's when we'll let them in. We can make them some food and we've some space in the storeroom for them to sleep. We've got a load of old bean bags they can use as pillows!"

“This is really brilliant Cyril. This is going to make a huge difference,” smiled Ben. “I need to go now but I’ll be back tomorrow.”

“Ok boss, see you then.”

Chapter Thirty

"Auntie Mo, Auntie Mo!" cried Ben as he burst through the door.

Mo removed her apron and came rushing over. "What is it Ben? Are you ok?"

After thinking long and hard on the way home, Ben had decided that he had to tell Mo everything. "I'm ok Mo but please sit down, I need to speak to you."

Sat at the dinner table, enjoying a delicious homemade cottage pie with peas and broccoli, Ben told Mo absolutely everything. It was like turning on a garden hose for the first time; the information came flooding out of the young boy. Mo gasped as Ben told her all about Mike and his secret meetings with the directors and Penelope Weston. She cooed as Ben went on to tell her all about Tony and how much of a nice man he was. There were scowls and fist-slams on the table as she learnt that Mike had fired the old man. This was followed by panic as he brought her up to speed on the true scale of financial trouble that Toy Co was in. Then tears arrived when Ben told her about Vince Howler and the awful things he'd said to him. Finally, the tears turned into a mild howl as she learnt about Gruff and Terry and the smashed window. Inconsolable, Mo's kind face was dripping wet with tears. "Oh my baby Ben, why haven't you told me any of this? You poor thing!"

"Because you'd get like this," explained Ben, putting his hand on hers. "I didn't want to upset you."

"Well what are we going to do now?" asked Mo, blowing her nose.

Ben smiled. "Come on Mo, let's go. I have a plan."

*** CEO ***

The most accurate way to describe Tony's house would be to liken it to a neat white box. With its cute Georgian windows, proud front door, hanging baskets either side, and a white picket fence, it was clear that the owner took pride in his home. "Oh this is pretty", commented Mo as Ben knocked on the door. "Are you sure Tony lives here?" she asked hesitantly.

"I'm sure," winked Ben.

They heard footsteps and the sound of keys. Tony appeared, his face gaunt. "Ben, what are you doing here?" he asked, his eyes wide. "How did you know I lived here?"

Ben smiled. "I'm the CEO, I know where my employees live!"

Tony gave a wry smile. "But I'm not an employee now Ben, I was fired."

"Well we'll see about that!" said Mo, edging into the conversation. "Hi Tony, I'm Ben's Auntie. Call me Mo."

The old man's face lit up, he coiffed his grey hair and cleared his throat. "Oh hello Mo, lovely to meet you," he blushed. "Come in, come in."

Inside, Tony's house was the same as the exterior. It was immaculate and very cosy with wooden beams straddling the low ceilings. Ben and his auntie took a seat on the sofa as Tony brought in tea and biscuits and orange juice for Ben.

"Is that your wife?" asked Mo, nodding to a photo on the fireplace.

"Yes my late wife Mary. She passed away the day I retired," he said bitterly.

"Oh I'm sorry to hear that Tony, she's beautiful," replied Mo.

"I've got nothing now," sighed Tony as he took a seat opposite. "Just my beloved Dixie."

"Who's Dixie?" asked Ben.

Tony managed a half smile. "My dog, she's sleeping in the garden at the moment."

"So what happened?" asked Ben. "Why did Mike fire you?"

Tony told Ben and Mo about the meeting in which Mike's idea for a toy was rejected by the directors. He went on to explain how Mike was clearly struggling and finally that he'd accidentally knocked coffee over his papers.

Mo chuckled. "I wish I was there to see that!"

"It was quite funny actually," admitted Tony, a smile returning to his face. "But then about half an hour after the meeting, Mike came to see me."

"What did he say?" asked Ben.

"He told me I was too old to work there and fired me," he replied, the sadness returning. "He said that Toy Co needed to look to the future and that they needed fresh blood."

"What a pillock!" wailed Mo.

"What a plonker!" cried Ben. He leaped from the sofa and paced the room, the floorboards creaking with every step. "This has to stop! We have to save Toy Co. And Tony, you will have your job back!"

"But how?" asked Tony. "The company is struggling. Mike is in charge. I've been fired. Christmas is less than two months away."

Ben smiled. "Do you have a pen and paper Tony?"

Chapter Thirty One

Yawning as the clock struck midnight, Ben glanced at Mo snoring gently on the sofa. A tiny lamp gave just enough light for Ben and Tony, crouched over the dining room table, to work on their designs. "So if we make the eyes a bit bigger," whispered Ben. "That should almost be it."

Ben, Tony and Mo had been hard at work for over five hours, hatching a plan to save Toy Co. After a delicious feast of homemade pizza and sweet potato wedges, which Tony rustled up in the kitchen, the young boy and old man continued into the night as exhaustion finally got the better of Mo. Dixie slept peacefully by the roaring fire as the windows rattled from the battering rain. Ben was exhausted but buzzing, he was running on adrenaline.

"I think they look wonderful Ben," said Tony. "This collection is a timeless classic!"

Ben smiled. “Thanks Tony, I do think toys need to go back to basics.”

“Well young man, now we need to prepare a business plan,” explained Tony, pouring more tea from the pot.

“What do you mean by business plan?” asked Ben.

Opening his laptop, Tony explained, “a business plan includes important information about how to launch a new product. It provides details on how much it costs to make, how much you can sell it for, and how you will promote the product.”

“Wow that sounds like a lot of work,” said Ben, rubbing his eyes.

“It shouldn’t take too long, I’ve done a few of these in the past,” winked Tony.

After carrying out some online research, the pair discovered that children were buying less toys than ever before. “Why is that?” asked Tony.

"Simple," smiled Ben. "Toys are too complicated now. Children need to use their imagination. That's why we need to go back to basics. Make toys that are loveable, high quality and that last a lifetime."

Tony could only admire the boy's maturity; he was wise beyond his years.

Chapter Thirty Two

Ben often wondered why an hour in class felt like two hours. And why an hour at the weekend felt like ten minutes. But today was excruciatingly long. The night before, Ben had stayed up until 2am with Tony (and Mo) to hatch a plan to save Toy Co. Tony told Ben that the last thing he learnt before he was fired was that Mike would be meeting the directors at 4pm later that afternoon - Ben literally couldn't wait to surprise them. Despite not having dealt with the loss of his Mum and Dad, Ben felt better than he had in a long time. He felt confident and able to deal with setbacks. He was answering questions in class and had even started to make friends. After a long day of double maths and geography with Mr Furrilip (Ben noticed that he'd had cauliflower cheese for lunch as the stringy cheese refused to let go of his moustache), the bell finally rang. Ben jumped up like a cheetah and headed for the school gates. Bursting through the double doors and hurtling down the path, Ben was just about to hop on his skateboard when Vince and his gang appeared. "Well well well, if it isn't Big Ben," snarled Vince. "You're getting a bit cocky lately aren't you?"

Just when he thought everything was getting better at school, Vince happens.

"Vince, what do you want?" asked Ben, exasperated. "Look I haven't got time for this. I need to go."

Vince edged forward. "You can go when I say you can you little snot bag. Just you remember who is the boss around here. You may be getting a little too confident. Just remember I can always knock you back down to size."

Ben shrugged. "Vince, do what you want. I don't care!"

"You don't care eh?" sneered the bully.

Ben moved closer to Vince this time, making him step back in surprise. "Listen Vince, I know the reason why you are like you are. Because your Dad doesn't pay you enough attention."

"That's none of your business you little squirt!" screamed Vince, shoving Ben backwards.

"Well actually it is my business because you are being horrible to me," replied Ben calmly. "Take it from someone who doesn't have a Mum or Dad. Just speak to your Dad. Tell him how you feel."

Vince's head dropped, his eyes focussed on the ground. One his friends affectionately placed his hand on his shoulder.

"Get off will you!" cried Vince, shrugging him off.

Ben took a softer stance. "Look Vince, I've got to go. But why don't you go and see your Dad now. Wherever he is, even if he's at work. Go and see him."

And with that, Ben walked away leaving Vince and his friends in the middle of the field.

Chapter Thirty Three

"Good afternoon everyone," announced Mike, straightening his tie. After the nightmare meeting the day before, in which the directors had disagreed with everything he said, as well as the IT issues and spilt coffee, Mike had spent the evening giving himself a makeover and pampering session. He had treated himself to a spray tan, moisturized his skin, dyed his hair, and bought a new suit. Unfortunately for Mike, the spray tan was more 'streaky' than 'spray'.

"Are you ok Mike?" asked Mrs Chopra. "You look a little..."

"…orange?" chuckled Mr Howler.

As you know, Mike was notorious for telling lies. "I'm fine Mrs Chopra, thank you for your concern," he smiled. "Just got a bit sunburnt last night."

"Sunburnt? It's October!" wailed Mr Howler incredulously.

"I have a beautiful balcony in my penthouse apartment," said Mike proudly. "It's a sun trap up there."

"More like sun cr..." said Mr Owen, stopping mid-sentence.

"Did the sun dye your hair as well?" asked Mrs Chopra. "You look a little less...grey today."

"No," answered Mike. "It's just grown overnight."

“Bleedin’ heck!” wailed Mr Howler with a hearty cackle. “In the space of 24 hours your hair and skin have naturally changed colour? What the heck are you eating?”

“It’s just the way I am,” replied Mike, dead serious. “Anyway, please can we change the subject?” He sat down and ruffled his papers. “I know yesterday’s meeting was challenging but I’m sure you appreciate that we are in a difficult situation as a company.” He took a sip of water. “We need to come to a decision on whether we sell Toy Co to Toy Universe. You received the information overnight. It would be great to hear what you think.”

Mike surveyed the directors around the table. The atmosphere was tense, their relationship strained.

“I’m sad to say this,” sighed Mrs Chopra. “But after careful thought, I think we should sell the company. We are facing a very difficult Christmas period and I don’t see things improving after that.”

“If we can get £300million we should take it,” added Mr Owen.

“What about the employees?” asked Mr Howler, his bushy eyebrows raising. “It wasn’t clear whether they will be losing their jobs or moving to the new company.”

Mike shifted in his seat. “It all depends really,” he said awkwardly. “We have no control over that. Now if you’d like to sign the paperwork then we can ask our lawyers to take care of the rest.” He handed out a document which each director then read in silence. Mike watched eagerly before letting out a quiet sigh when the directors eventually signed the papers.

“What about you Mike?” asked Mrs Chopra, sliding the paper back to him. “Surely this means you won’t have a job?”

Mike took another gulp of water. “Well, I have been offered a job at Toy Universe,” he explained. “They’re making me Managing Director.”

Mr Owen shot up, his red head skimming the low-hanging lamp above. "What?" he cried, his face as red as his hair. "You've been offered a job at Toy Universe, but all our employees may lose theirs?"

Mike smiled. "This is the world of business Mr Owen. You know that."

"And what else have you been offered?" asked Mrs Chopra angrily.

"That is private business between me and Toy Universe," replied Mike mockingly.

"As directors we have a right to know!" demanded Mr Howler, slamming his fist on the table.

At that moment, the door burst open. Ben marched in wearing a suit, the same suit he wore to his Mum and Dad's funeral. Only this time he wore a powerful blue tie to go with it. His hair was brushed into a side parting, he felt great. He was doing this for his parents.

"Ben? Again! What are you doing here?" wailed Mike.

Chapter Thirty Four

"Good afternoon ladies and gentlemen, I'm Ben Hamley, CEO of Toy Co. It's a pleasure to meet you all." The young boy sat at the head of the table next to his uncle. He placed his briefcase on the table and opened it. "Now, I hear that my parents' company is in trouble. And I've come to save it."

The directors watched in silence.

"Ben, you shouldn't be here," hissed Mike. "Please, now run along home will you."

"Mike, this is my company and I will stay here for as long as I want," said Ben confidently. "By the way, have you dyed your hair?"

The directors chuckled.

Ben's short frame meant his shoulders were just about visible above the boardroom table. "Ladies and gentlemen, for the last 12 months Toy Co has struggled." He paused and gave Mike a knowing look.

"That's because we've lost touch with what our customers want. All the while our competitors are launching ahead and taking market share."

The directors nodded in agreement.

"And how would you know what our customers want?" snapped Mike.

"Simple, I am one," smiled Ben. "In case you haven't noticed, I am eleven years old. I am the typical customer of Toy Co." He sat up straight in his chair. "Well...maybe I'm a little bit old now but I still know what kids want because I am one!"

The directors all looked at each other and nodded.

"Tony!" called Ben suddenly. "Please can you give me a hand."

Tony entered with Mo closely behind.

"Tom, what are you doing here?" asked Mike furiously. "I fired you the other day! And Mo, you should be at home!"

"With all due respect Mike, my name is Tony. Not Tom. Ben has asked me to help him in his capacity as CEO of Toy Co."

"But I'm the CEO of Toy Co!" cried Mike.

"No you're not," spat Mo. "You're only in charge because Mr and Mrs Hamley wanted to spend more time with Ben last summer. If they were still around you wouldn't be CEO. This is Ben's company now."

Mike gave a heinous laugh before slamming his fist on the table. "You silly fools! You think this is your company? We've just sold it to Toy Universe!"

Chapter Thirty Five

A wave of heat swept through Ben. “What? That can’t be! You have no right to sell the company without telling me!”

“But that’s where you’re wrong little boy, because I do,” smirked Mike. “My good friend Mrs Weston helped make sure of that. Always good to have a lawyer on your side!”

The door opened suddenly. Penelope Weston entered, full of swagger and sophistication, wearing a marvellous red power suit, matching dangly earrings, and holding her obligatory coffee like a fashion accessory. “Yes Mike it is,” she said. “Which is why I’m here for Ben. What you asked me to do is illegal.”

A bead of sweat sloped down Mike’s forehead. “But… Penelope… I thought we had a deal? I would give you £10million if you helped me sell the company.”

"Mike, there are more important things in life than money and besides, I have plenty already!" she laughed before taking a seat. "Anyway, Ben is like a nephew to me," she continued, sweeping the long dark hair from her face. "I would never do such a thing. How you could do this to your nephew is downright awful."

Mike stood up and kicked a chair sending it flying. He began pacing the room, breathing heavily. "All my life I've lived in my stupid brother's shadow," he wailed dramatically. "Even when we were children my Mum preferred him to me. All I've ever wanted was to be loved and respected! Is that too much to ask?" He sighed and looked at the ceiling. "This was my chance to make something of myself."

"Well you've certainly done that now," sneered Mo, her cheeks wobbling with anger. "I've never trusted you."

"Oh shut it old lady, you're always nosing into other people's business," snarled Mike. "Just because you've got nothing better to do!"

Tony launched towards Mike. "How dare you speak to Mo like that, have you no manners?" he cried shaking with fury. "Mo is a beautiful and kind lady who is looking after your nephew while you try to rip him off!"

"Oh be quiet Tom," said Mike.

"TONY!" cried everyone.

Mr Howler stood up. "Well, it's safe to say that we have never experienced a board meeting like this! I think I speak on behalf of the directors when I say Mike...you're fired."

Mike spread his arms wide and cried, "you can't fire me! Toy Co doesn't exist anymore. We've sold it. It's too late!"

"Sorry Mike, you're wrong again," said Penelope, a smile on her face. "Those contracts I sent you aren't legally binding. They are worthless."

Mike turned pale as if he was about to faint. He leaned back against the wall and slid down it like a slug.

"It's over Mike," said Ben.

Chapter Thirty Six

With Mike slumped in the corner, sobbing quietly like a wet puppy left out in the rain, Ben now commanded the head of table. "Now ladies and gentlemen, if you could all take a seat. I would like to finish my presentation...".

"Dad!" came a familiar voice.

Ben looked up and was shocked to see Vince Howler in the doorway, bedraggled and out of breath.

"Vince, what are you doing here?" asked Ben, taken aback.

"What are you doing here more like?" snarled the bully.

"Son?" gasped Mr Howler, equally as shocked as the two boys.

"Dad... I've come to see you...I...I...never see you... you're always working...I miss you," stuttered Vince, his bottom lip wobbling.

"Oh son, come here will you," said Mr Howler, tears in his eyes. He stood up and approached the boy. "I'm sorry Vince, ever since your Mum left I've thrown myself into work. When in fact I should have devoted all of my time to you. I'm sorry son."

"That's ok Dad," replied Vince, cuddling him.

Ben couldn't believe it - Vince Howler's Dad was Mr Howler! Of course - it made perfect sense! Ben had never seen Vince like this before. He almost wanted to give him a hug.

The directors burst into a round of applause.

"I'm sorry everyone," blubbered Mr Howler, choking back the tears. "This is some board meeting!"

Ben stood up. "This is what Toy Co is all about; it's about family and taking care of others. Welcome Vince!"

Vince smiled sheepishly and took a seat at the table next to his Dad.

"Family? You have no idea what family is!" blasted Mike, suddenly returning to his feet. "All of you are pathetic! The lot of you! Pathetic!" He turned to leave, his face twisted like an olive tree. "You'll regret this Ben, I mean it!"

Mike opened the door and screamed – it was Gruff and Terry - carrying guns.

Chapter Thirty Seven

Grunting and slobbering all over the place, Gruff and Terry entered the boardroom like a pair of Bloodhounds, leaving a trail of saliva in their wake. Dressed in skin-tight white jeans and t-shirt, no doubt in an attempt to resemble their heroes the **Mafia***, it was hardly the most flattering choice of outfit for their chubby physiques; they looked more like **Right Said Fred**** dressed up as **ABBA**** after over-indulging on Swedish meatballs from **Ikea*****; legendary Italian gangsters they were certainly not.

Note from author: *warning! If you don't know what the Mafia is, and would like to find out, please don't bother if you like horses.*

Note from author part two: *if you don't know who Right Said Fred and Abba are please don't worry; you can find out from a range of sources; please feel free to Ask Jeeves, or Professor Google, or perhaps you could even speak to a family member who is at least twenty* *years older than you (ok so the last option may be taking things a bit too far).*

Note from author part three: *if you have never heard of Ikea, don't ask your parents about it (you can thank me later).*

"Well look who we 'ave 'ere!" barked Gruff, phlegm flying everywhere. "If it isn't Mike havin' afternoon tea wiv 'is mates. Ain't this cosy?"

It was all too much for Mike, he collapsed to the ground. "Please," he begged. "I'll do anything. Please… just leave me alone!"

"Ave ya' been on 'oliday Mikey boy? growled Terry, casually nudging him with his boot. "Ya' best not 'ave left the country withou' tellin' us!"

"What ya' on abou' now Terry?" sighed Gruff. "What do ya' mean 'as he been on 'oliday?"

"Look at 'im…look at 'is face…ee looks a little..."

"ORANGE!" cried everyone.

The gangsters cackled at the pathetic heap at their feet. Gruff cracked his knuckles, the sound popping around the silent boardroom. Ben flinched, he hated it when people did that. Studying the terrified directors sat around the table, Gruff laughed, "well, ain't this an ugly bunch?" With his gun, he surveyed them one-by-one, everyone ducking instinctively as the weapon was pointed in their direction. Though it wasn't clear whether they were ducking due to the possibility of being shot, or if they were simply doing their best to avoid the spray of spit flying their way. Vince clung tightly to his Dad - Mo let out a sob - Tony held her close - Mr Owen stared into space - Mrs Chopra kept her head down - Penelope drank her coffee.

Terry bent down so his face was in breathing distance to Mike. "All we want is our money," he growled.

"And me diamond," added Gruff.

"Diamond?" asked Ben.

"Shut it you," spat Gruff, literally. "You're the little rich boy aren't ya? The one who was wiv Mike outside that stupid posh lawyer's office!"

“No not me,” said Ben, sinking into his chair.

“I beg your pardon?” wailed Penelope.

Gruff marched over to Ben and effortlessly dragged the young boy from his chair. He raised his weapon. “Listen Mike, I want me diamond and dosh or this little sprout will be brown bread.”

“Take me take me!” screamed Mo.

“You should never eat bread after lunchtime,” commented Penelope. “Sprouts are ok though, good for digestion.”

“Shut it you!” barked Terry.

Mike got up from the floor and pulled himself together. “Easy now fellas, come on follow me.”

Chapter Thirty Eight

In the world of business, there are all sorts of strange and peculiar happenings; especially in meetings. If you ever find yourself sat round a boardroom table, it's worth remembering the five golden rules:

Rule number 1: no flatulence (I'm sorry I didn't want to be rude and include the word 'fart' in this book)

Rule number 2: whatever you do, before attending a meeting *do not* eat garlic bread, raw garlic, or basically any food that contains garlic

Rule number 3: no spitting when talking (or at any time during the meeting)

Rule number 4: no **shouting**

Rule number 5: and finally, in under no circumstances should anyone ever bring a gun or any form of weapon to a meeting (or anywhere else for that matter)

Gruff and Terry had managed to break almost all of the rules within minutes of entering the room. Luckily for Ben and his fellow hostages, they had yet to experience them breaking (wind) the first rule. With the boardroom getting crowded now, the air was stuffy enough as it was, the last thing they needed was for the gangsters to let off some steam. With everyone stunned into silence and scared witless, and with Mike offering to lead the way to the precious goods, Gruff was itching to get moving. "Righ' everyone, line up along the wall in single file NOW!" he barked, practically bouncing on the spot. "Terry, go find some rope or sumfink' will ya'. We need to tie this lot up. GO ON THEN! QUICK!"

Terry scarpered out of the door and returned a few moments later with a microwave-sized cardboard box.

"Gaawden Bennet! What the flamin' 'eck is that?" spat Gruff. "I asked for rope not a box ya idiot! How the flippin' 'eck are they gonna fit in there?"

Ben had always been under the impression that Terry was the most stupid of the two; now he wasn't so sure.

"It's all I could find boss," explained Terry bashfully. He ripped the box open and emptied its contents onto the boardroom table. Out spilled a gaggle of toy rubber snakes - bright yellow with orange and brown specks.

"SNAKES! SNAKES! TOY RUBBER SNAKES!" wailed Gruff, stomping his feet like a toddler having a tantrum. "WHAT WE SUPPOSED TO DO WITH THOSE FINGS?" He kicked a chair sending it flying against the wall, narrowly missing Mo who wept in response. Gruff began to walk in a circle on the spot while muttering to himself. Ben shivered watching such bizarre behaviour. The gangster stopped suddenly laughed loudly, "mind you Terry, I always knew ya' were a slippery character!" Grabbing a rubber snake, he stretched it like an elastic band to test its strength. "Actually, I 'ave an idea…"

“What’s that boss?” asked Terry. “Put the kid in the box? What we gonna do wiv the rest of ‘em?”

“Not that ya stupid idiot, I meant tie ‘em up with the snakes!”

“Boss, ya’ a genius!” cooed Terry.

“Shut up and tie ‘em up will ya!”

Grabbing a bundle of rubber snakes, Terry followed his boss’s orders and tied the hostages together with their hands behind their backs. Within minutes, Ben, Mo, Tony, Mr Howler, Vince, Mrs Chopra, Penelope, and Mr Owen, formed one long chain of people.

With his pistol pressed firmly against Mike’s cheek, Gruff barked, “we’re not tying you up sunshine…you’ve got work to do! Now take me to me bleedin’ diamond…where is she?”

“Downstairs,” replied Mike meekly, his legs shaking. By now, his sweaty face had washed away almost all of the fake tan leaving an orange stain on his shirt.

"Well, what ya' waitin' for! GET A MOVE ON!" boomed Gruff.

Mike whimpered as he led the convoy of hostages out from the boardroom and down the corridor. Gruff and Terry walked alongside them, their pistols following their every move.

Chapter Thirty Nine

After a painfully slow walk from the boardroom, in which Ben and his fellow hostages trudged down eight flights of stairs in single-file with their hands tied together by rubber snakes, they eventually reached the ground floor where Gruff and Terry herded them like cattle into the very centre of Toy Co - a large circular space with the store's famous logo emblazoned across the wooden floor. Ben surveyed his surroundings, it felt weird being in the store when it was closed; with no customers and background music; the place felt empty. Probably because it *was* empty. From where the hostages were huddled, aisles split off in all directions, each full to the brim with magical toys of a specific kind. To the right was the robot aisle, to the left was dinosaurs, behind was cars, planes and trains, and straight ahead was the teddy bear section. Towering silhouettes of toy-displays stood proudly like statues everywhere he looked. Up above, industrial-sized security lights offered a dull glare making the store feel half asleep.

Pacing up and down like an angry gorilla, Gruff was in a foul mood. "Right, you lot SIT DOWN!" he barked suddenly.

The hostages followed his orders and sat cross-legged in the floor.

Mike was spared the misfortune of being tied up with the hostages. Sadly for him, instead of a rubber snake tied around his wrists he had a loaded pistol digging into his forehead. Gruff turned to him. "Right, where's me diamond ya scrawny little weasel?"

"Near the teddy bears," whimpered Mike.

Gruff grabbed Mike by his collar and ragged him like a doll, the gangster's ginormous gold rings pressing into his pointy chin. "WHAT? YOU LEFT £1MILLION AND ME DIAMOND IN A SHOP? ARE YA' AN IDIOT OR SUMFINK?"

"YES!" everyone cried.

"It was an accident," wept Mike. "When you told me to hide the money and diamond, I thought what better hiding place than a toy store?" He looked at Gruff for unity on this point, but he clearly wasn't getting any. He continued, "the store was closed and I thought I was alone." Anger consumed his face for a moment. "Then I heard someone coming, I heard whistling, so I panicked and stuffed them in a teddy bear. It was that stupid Cyril. He came out of nowhere and caught me by surprise." His voice began to croak with the pressure of Gruff's hands around his neck. "I turned my back for a second and the bear was gone."

Like a sack of sweet potatoes, Mike collapsed in a heap as Gruff released his grip.

"So that's why you were caught stealing a teddy bear!" cried Ben, a sense of triumph in his voice. "You were trying to find the diamond!"

Mike didn't reply. What could he say? Without even bothering to stand up, he slithered across the floor a few metres until he reached a monumental display of teddy bears, piled high on top of each other in a mountain at least as tall as Gruff. A sign above it read 'Talkin' Teddies', presumably because the teddies could talk.

On his hands and knees, Mike began to ransack the bears in search of the money and diamond. Each time he discovered a teddy that was penniless and diamond-less, he let out a heavy sigh and nonchalantly tossed it over his shoulder. In doing so, he unwittingly activated the teddy's voice function. Within minutes, Mike was surrounded by a crowd of teddy bears talking gibberish.

"Hello my name is 'Talkin' Teddy!'"
"Hello, my friend, can I give you a hug?"
"Talkin Teddy is here for you!"
"You're my best friend!"
"Will you play with me?"

Meanwhile, Tony and Mo, still tied up with the rest of the hostages, were enjoying a quiet chuckle between themselves as they watched a very sweaty Mike frantically search for the elusive bear.

"Those bears sound more like parrots!" whispered Tony. "They just repeat themselves!"

Mo giggled for a moment then said, "I know, they don't stop rabbiting on!"

"I would be lion if I said I wanted one!" sniggered Tony.

"Well, maybe I'll get you one for Christmas. I'll see what I have in my piggy bank!" winked Mo.

"Are you sure? I think they're quite deer!" chuckled Tony.

Oblivious to Tony and Mo's mild flirting over animal puns, Ben's mind was elsewhere. "No wonder they're on sale!" he whispered, dead serious. "We'll get rid of those things when I'm in charge. Who wants to listen to that racket all day?"

Tony and Mo glanced at each other and smiled. Ben was right, the teddies didn't stop talking and now that Mike had rifled through an army of them, the sound was deafening.

"What ya doin' ya rodent?" barked Gruff, his pistol aimed at Mike.

“I’m looking for the bear!” exclaimed Mike, trying to make himself heard over the cacophony of talking teddies.

“What? Ya’ don’t know which bear it is?” wailed Gruff, his gun shaking with fury.

Ben interrupted. “Why would you leave the money and diamond here all of this time Mike?” he shouted. “You’ve had months to look for it! What’s going on?”

“Oi, we’re askin’ the questions, shut it kid,” growled Terry. “We’re the gangsters in this gaff. Ain’t that right boss?”

“Shut it Terry. The kid has a point,” replied Gruff, thinking for a moment. “Why would he leave the diamond here all this time?”

Ben poked his tongue out at Terry.

Sitting up on his knees, hands on hips, Mike glanced up, his thinning hair stuck to his lunar forehead. “Because I haven’t had a chance!” he cried, throwing his arms in the air. “I’ve been running this stupid company that’s why.”

"You couldn't run a bath!" cried Mr Howler.

"Come on Mike, tell us where this diamond is!" heckled Mrs Chopra. "I'm dying to see it!"

"SHUT IT! THE LOT O' YA!" growled Gruff. He prowled round the pile of teddies surrounding Mike. "Why would he leave the diamond 'ere all this time? What if the teddy was bought by a child?"

Ben wasn't sure if Mike was playing bluff. Why would he hide a huge wad of cash and a diamond in a teddy bear and leave it on display? It didn't make sense. Unless he was just stupid? But surely no one is that stupid?

"I didn't know that did I?" wailed Mike, resuming his search. "I stuffed it in a teddy and then it simply vanished."

"What did the teddy look like?" asked Ben.

"I don't know," huffed Mike. "I didn't take much notice."

“YA’ DIDN’T TAKE ANY NOTICE WHEN YA’ STUFFED A LOAD O’ MY DOSH AND DIAMOND IN IT?” screamed Gruff, he was foaming at the mouth which was normal for him but on this occasion even his spit looked angry.

“No it just seemed to vanish all by itself,” pleaded Mike. “Honest!”

“Oh come on Mike, you lied about stealing the teddy bear all those months ago” cried Mo. “How can a bear just vanish?”

“He lied about dying his hair as well,” chuckled Mr Owen.

“And his suntan,” bellowed Mrs Chopra.

The hostages laughed.

At that moment, something in Ben’s mind clicked. “Wait a minute, I think for once Mike may just be telling the truth.”

"Thank you Ben...I think," said Mike, pulling a face.

"What do ya' mean boy? Come on spit it out!" boomed Gruff.

"I think we have enough spit in here as it is," said Mr Howler under his breath.

His fellow hostages giggled.

"Oi! What did you say?" barked Gruff, edging towards him.

"Nothing Mr Gruff," answered Mr Howler, like a naughty schoolboy.

"Well keep quiet then," said Gruff. He turned to Ben. "Come on boy, what do ya' mean?"

"I think I know where the money is," said Ben.

Chapter Forty

"No you don't," scowled Mike. "How would you know?"

"More chance of him knowing where the money and diamonds are than you," laughed Penelope. "You're the worst thief ever!"

"Where are they boy?" asked Gruff, grabbing him by his tie.

"I'll only tell you if you let everyone go. And tell me why Mike is involved," demanded Ben.

Gruff was warming to Ben, he admired his courage. "Listen boy, if ya' bring me the cash and the diamond, ya' can all go. But am not tellin' ya' why ya' paffetic uncle is involved. Cos' he's comin' wiv us."

Despite all of the terrible things Mike had done, Ben didn't want his uncle to get hurt. He felt kind of sorry for him. There he was, sat on the floor among a heap of talking teddy bears in a sorry state. "I know my uncle is useless, but don't hurt him. He's harmless. I will lead you to the money, just let us all go."

"Thank you," muttered Mike, again carrying a perplexed look.

Gruff let out a heavy sigh. "Fair 'nuff, just show us where they are, and we'll leave."

"And one more condition," said Ben.

"What's that?"

"You put down your guns."

"Put down our Lady of Bristol's? Who do ya' fink ya' are?" barked Gruff, jabbing Ben in the shoulder with an extremely fat finger. "Ya' pushin' ya' luck rich boy."

"I beg your pardon," cried Penelope suddenly. "I know the Lady of Bristol, I had dinner with her last week. She's not here is she?"

Mr Howler nudged Penelope and whispered, "Lady of Bristol means pistol in Cockney rhyming slang, pistol as in a gun."

“Oh,” replied the lawyer. “Well I once went clay-pigeon shooting with the Lady of Bristol, so I guess that makes sense!”

“KEEP THE NOISE DOWN OVER THERE!” growled Gruff, his chubby finger still firmly pressed into Ben’s shoulder.

“I’m sorry Gruff,” replied Ben. “I’m just trying to do my best for everyone. Come on, untie me and I’ll show you.”

“RIGHT EVERYONE, ON YA’ FEET NOW!” shouted Terry, as he untied Ben.

It was a mighty struggle for seven people to stand up at precisely the same time with their hands tied behind their backs (and to each other). Especially for Mo and Tony who were much older than the rest of the hostages. Despite being in fine health, being held captive was starting to take its toll on the elderly pair. After much grunting and groaning, the group eventually rose to its feet. Ben led the way towards a sign that read

'Robots' with Gruff and the hostages following closely behind while Terry kept his beady eye on Mike at the back of the pack.

"Tell me where we're goin' boy," demanded Gruff. "Ya' best not be lyin'."

"I'm not Gruff," smiled Ben. He continued down the aisle, passing hundreds of incredible robots on display. Ben noticed that there were robots of all different varieties; robotic dinosaurs, birds, cars; he even spotted a robot butler that tidied your room! He stopped as they reached the end of the aisle. "Ah, here we are." He turned to face the group, "here's my friend Mr Monkey. Mike, does he look familiar?"

His uncle's face tightened. "Erm...that does look familiar."

There was a moment of silence.

"Ya' don't mean..." said Gruff quietly.

"Yes that's right Gruff," smiled Ben. "Mike thought he'd hidden the money and diamond in a teddy bear when in fact he'd hidden them in Mr Monkey!"

"What an absolute moron!" wailed Mr Howler.

Everyone started laughing at Mike.

"How do ya' know this boy?" asked Terry angrily.

Approaching Mr Monkey to switch him on, Ben replied, "because I remember being greeted by Mr Monkey a couple of weeks ago. When Mike said the teddy vanished, then it must have been a teddy that could move."

"Bravo young Ben!" cried Penelope.

"Well done poppet!" hollered Mo.

"SHUT IT THE LOT O' YA'!" scowled Gruff.

Mr Monkey suddenly jolted into life and approached Gruff. "Can I help you sir?"

"Yeah give me me bleedin' money and diamond!" growled the gangster.

"He can't understand you, Boss, he's a robot," explained Terry deadpan.

"I KNOW THAT YA' STUPID IMBECILE! NOW JUST GET ME ME

MONEY AND DIAMOND!" barked Gruff, covering Mr Monkey in phlegm.

Terry grabbed Mr Monkey, span him round and opened the compartment in his back. He shoved his hand inside and rummaged around. "Here it is!" he cried as he pulled out a brown envelope stuffed with cash.

"Good. Where's the diamond?" asked Gruff impatiently.

"It should be 'ere somewhere," strained Terry, his hand still inside Mr Monkey. "Ah...I fink I got it...it's definitely here…I can feel it…I fink..." And with that, Terry yanked his hand out of Mr Monkey's back with such force that he accidentally let go of the huge diamond, the size of a tennis ball, which flew through the air. Ben and the hostages watched open-mouthed as the diamond sailed in slow motion across the store, hurtling over the aisles of toys and narrowly missing a life-size T-Rex in the dinosaur section. The diamond was a thing of beauty; like a flying mini-disco ball, its magnificent body sparkled in the reflection of the giant security lights. The diamond continued its trajectory towards Mike who was waiting with baited breath, his eyes focussed solely on the flying fortune. There was a collective gasp from Gruff, Terry and the hostages as Mike suddenly arched his body and spectacularly dived into the air to perform an acrobatic catch. He immediately returned to his feet gripping the diamond tightly.

Chapter Forty One

"Ok Mikey boy, 'and it over," ordered Gruff, his Lady of Bristol on display.

"No!" called Mike, feeling pleased with himself. "This is mine, after everything I've done for you. It's the least I deserve!"

Facing the man holding his diamond, the very diamond that he'd been searching for months, Gruff was surprisingly calm. He gave Mike a cold stare, his tiny blue eyes not blinking once. After a few moments, he broke the silence. "Ok then Mike, if that's the way it's gonna be, we'll take our own diamond," he said quietly. He grabbed Ben suddenly. "Am sorry boy, but I 'ave got to do this." He shoved the pistol into the back of the young boy's head. "Give me the diamond Mike, or ya' little nephew gets it."

"You think I care about him?" laughed Mike.

"How could you?" wept Mo.

"Oh shut it old lady," snapped Mike.

"Just you wait until I get my hands on you," shouted Tony, shaking with anger as he tried to wriggle free from the chain of hostages.

"SIT DOWN AND SHUT UP!"

blasted Gruff.

With Mo, Tony, Penelope, Vince, Mr Howler, Mrs Chopra and Mr Owen lined up on the floor, sat cross-legged and tied together with the pesky rubber snakes, in front of them, a tense stand-off took place. Mike, surrounded by an army of teddy bears sprawled out on the floor, lovingly cradled the enormous diamond as if it was a newborn baby. Ten feet away, Gruff held Ben like a ragdoll. The store was dark now and with the exception of the sound of heavy breathing and Mo trying her best to sob quietly, the place was eerily quiet.

"Mike, just give me diamond back," ordered Gruff as he ushered Ben forward with his pistol.

"No!" shouted Mike, his eyes manic. "It's all I've got now, just me and my precious baby!"

Mike began to back away slowly, his eyes focussed on the pistol pointing right at him. In doing so, he accidently tripped on a 'Talkin' Teddy'. "Aaargh!" he screamed as its voice activated. The shock made him stumble back and bump into a luminous life-size skeleton hanging from a Halloween display. "Aaargh!" he cried as the skeleton rattled from the impact.

"He's even scared ov a bag a' bones!" laughed Terry.

"I think that's his twin!" heckled Mr Howler.

"I doubt that," chuckled Mrs Chopra. "I think the skeleton has more brains."

"And a far superior taste in coffee," wailed Penelope despairingly.

"Do skeletons drink coffee?" asked Mrs Chopra.

"Coffee is very good for your bones dear," replied Penelope, her response as serious as the question.

"Oi shut it, the lot o' ya!" barked Gruff. "Ow many times do I 'ave to tell ya?" He edged closer towards Mike, shuffling Ben along like a chess piece. "There's nowhere to go Mikey boy, just give yasel' up. Just give me the diamond n' we'll leave ya' alone."

As quick as a flash, Mike stuffed the diamond into his suit jacket and leaped onto a jumbo-sized space hopper nearby. In one smooth motion, he made an almighty thrust on the space hopper, propelling him into the air and up onto a trampoline. With seemingly minimal effort, he took two powerful leaps on the trampoline and within a matter of seconds, Mike had high-jumped over the balcony and had landed on two feet on the mezzanine up above.

Mike was out of sight.

Chapter Forty Two

"GERRIM!" barked Gruff.

BANG! BANG! BANG!

Even though Mike was out of sight, Terry began to randomly fire shots at the balcony above. Scared witless, Mo let out an almighty cry and snuggled into Tony. In fact, everyone was scared. Up until now, this had been a thoroughly entertaining experience for the hostages considering the circumstances, but the sound of gun fire was a stark reminder that Gruff and Terry were nasty pieces of work.

Gruff scowled at his sidekick. "WHAT YA' WAITIN' FOR? GERRIM!" he screamed, his face scarlet with rage.

Following his boss's orders, Terry set off in pursuit of Mike. He ran towards the steps that led to the balcony. Not exactly being the most athletic of people, Terry was halfway up the steps when it became quickly apparent that they presented a bit of a challenge for him. Climbing each step at a snail's pace, Terry was clearly struggling. His boss was furious. "TERRY, WHAT THE 'ECK ARE YA' DOIN' YA' USELESS SLUG!"

Terry, now three quarters of the way up the spiralling staircase, turned around to reveal his bright red face. "It's me trousers boss, they're a bit tight. I can barely move!"

"I TOLD YA' T' BUY EXTRA LARGE YA' BAFOON!" Gruff was shaking with fury. Ben tried his best to avoid the spray of phlegm, but he failed, his hair and shoulders were covered in the stuff. With Mo still sobbing, and Tony doing his best to console her, the rest of the hostages began to enjoy the entertainment once again.

"Terry should try one of my smoothies," whispered Penelope. "He will lose a few pounds then."

"I think they've already lost a few pounds," laughed Mr Howler. "£1million!"

"No I meant pounds as in weight," replied Penelope seriously.

"OI! WHAT DID I SAY EARLIER?" barked Gruff, spinning Ben round to face them. He pressed the gun against the young boy's cheek. "STOP TALKIN! OTHERWISE THIS LITTLE BOY WILL BE BROWN BREAD!"

"Excuse me," said Penelope. "But why do you keep talking about brown bread? I much prefer an organic vegan multi-seed slow-baked gluten-free sourdough if I'm perfectly honest."

Gruff gave a throaty laugh. "Oh you posh people, you have no idea do ya? Brown bread means..."

BEEP! BEEEEEEP!

Out of nowhere, the lights of what looked like a very small car shone brightly on Gruff. "What the..."

"Leave 'em alone boyo!" called a voice.

BEEP! BEEEEEEP!

It was Cyril!

The security guard was squeezed ever so tightly into an electric toy car. He put his foot down, the tyres screeched, and the engine roared, as he hurtled towards the gangster. Although the car wasn't fast by any means, it did cause a distraction. Gruff span round to face the oncoming vehicle and raised his pistol. Just as he was about to pull the trigger he felt **WHACK!** on the back of his head. He loosened his grip on Ben before collapsing in a heap on the floor, his gun clattering to the ground.

"What the..." gasped Ben open-mouthed at the sight of Gruff unconscious. He turned and glowing like an angel in the bright lights of the toy car, there stood Hannah, holding a giant toy mallet.

"Hannah, you saved us!" cried Ben, running to give her a hug.

"No she hasn't," came a voice.

Ben turned and saw Terry and Mike heading down the stairs.

They were back.

Chapter Forty Three

"Give it up Terry," called Ben. "There's nowhere to go!"

Sweating as if he'd just ran a marathon, Terry guided Mike down the stairs with his pistol pressed against the man's head. "Oh yeah there is," he scoffed. "I got me diamond, now give me me dosh!"

"We haven't got the money," smirked Ben. "Gruff's got it." He nodded to Terry's boss flat out on the floor.

"Ha ha very funny freckle boy," mocked Terry. "NOW GIVE ME ME MONEY!"

Ben knelt down and searched inside Gruff's pockets before pulling out the brown envelope.

"Chuck it 'ere," urged Terry. "Quick."

"No," said Ben, hugging the envelope against his chest.

"No?" cried Terry, as him and Mike reached the bottom of the steps. "What do ya' mean no?"

"I mean no, you stole this from someone," said Ben, standing defiant. "And I'm not giving you it back until you tell me why Mike is involved."

"Just give him the money," screamed Mike, his face wet with sweat, tears and fake tan.

"Poppet," came a frail voice. Ben turned and saw Mo quietly sobbing. Her usually cheerful face gaunt. "Please just give him the money dear," she said softly.

"Ok then," sighed Ben, he begrudgingly threw the envelope over to Terry.

Terry gave a sinister cackle. "Right you lot, stay 'ere, don't move. Me and me toy boy 'ere are goin out on a date ain't we Mikey boy?"

"Please Terry, NO!" sobbed Mike, he fell to his knees and wept.

"Gerrup ya' little weasel," snarled Terry, jabbing Mike in the ribs with his boot. He looked at Ben. "First, we need to tie this little minstrel up don't we Benjamin?" Terry was in a jolly mood now that he had got what he wanted. "Go sit next to ya' grandad and grandma."

"Who?" asked Ben.

Terry nodded to Mo and Tony. "Those two coffin dodgers on the end. Whoever they are, go sit next to 'em, 'urry." In the corner of his eye, Terry spotted Cyril trying to escape. "Oi Squirrel, don't fink I've forgotten 'bout you eeever! Get over there wiv Big Ben." Terry faced Hannah. "And you street urchin, get over there."

Cyril crawled out from behind the Halloween display. He scurried over and together with Ben and the homeless girl, they duly obliged and followed the man's orders. They sat on the floor next to Tony, who was on the end of the hostage chain.

"Get up!" cried Terry, pulling a rubber snake dangling from his back pocket. "Always good to 'ave a spare rubber snake! Ya never know when ya might need one," he laughed as he tied Hannah,

Cyril and Ben together with their wrists behind their backs. He then tied Ben's hands to Tony's. "Ha ha! That's better," he cackled. "Now, let's get out ov 'ere. Come on Mikey, let's go."

"What about Gruff?" cried Ben. "Are you going to leave him? He's your boss!"

"I don't 'ave time to carry him out ov 'ere, 'e was always 'orrible to me anyway! Besides, it's double bubble for Tel Tel tonight!" he grinned, rubbing his hands.

"Is it now?" came a deep gravelly voice.

Terry turned round suddenly. "Boss," he said sheepishly. "I fought..."

"Ya' fought wrong ya' paffettik fool," growled Gruff, picking himself up from the floor. "Now give me what is mine."

Chapter Forty Four

Admittedly, Gruff wasn't in a brilliant position. Terry had the money, the diamond and more importantly a gun. He glanced at his weapon lying on the floor a few feet away before his eyes returned to Terry and Mike. He was just about to make a run for it when Mike performed a somersault roll and grabbed it. "My how the tables have turned," he grinned as he aimed the gun at Gruff.

Then Terry pointed his gun at Gruff.

"What's going on?" cried Ben.

"Yeah, what's goin' on?" growled Gruff, clearly shocked at this turn of events.

"You see Mr Gruff," began Mike. "Your friend here, good old Terry, is actually my friend."

Gruff looked at Terry who gave a sheepish nod.

"All of this time, we have been plotting to get our hands on the diamond," grinned Mike, edging around Gruff in a circle. "And now we finally have what is rightfully ours." He laughed loudly, the sound reverberating around the empty store.

"Terry, 'ow could ya?" pleaded Gruff, visibly upset. "I fought we were pals?"

"Am sorry boss," replied Terry, staring at the ground. "Yav always been so 'orrible to me." He looked at Mike. "This man is so kind and easy to work wiv. We've become more than friends 'aven't we Mike?"

"We certainly have my dear," cooed Mike with the kind of smile that Ben had never seen before.

"But I don't get it," cried Ben. "I still don't understand why you hid the diamond and the money in a teddy bear."

"Well young Benjamin," answered Mike, full of himself now. "Gruff and Terry gave me the diamond and cash as they knew the police were watching them." He looked at Terry. "That's when Terry and I came up with our plan. I would hide them in a teddy bear, and Terry would send his niece into the store to buy it." Clearly very proud of his idea, be went on, "unfortunately, stupid Squirrel the security guard over there disrupted me and when I turned round, the teddy was gone."

"But why are you involved with these people Mike?" asked Ben. "I don't understand?"

"Because Ben, sometimes in life you've got to take a shortcut to get you want," he grinned. "And what I want is to be rich! I want to be able to have so much money that I can swim in it!" he cried as he began pacing up and down. "So I can buy yachts, racing cars, mansions all around the world!" He paused for a moment then said menacingly, "I'm going to be so rich that I'm going to wipe my bum with £50 notes!"

"Talk about putting your money where your mouth is," muttered Mr Howler.

"Your bottom will get very sore doing that Mike," explained Mrs Chopra.

Mike's eyes were wild with excitement as Terry held aloft the diamond in the palm of his hand. Even in the faded light it glistened like a star. "You see boy? This beautiful rock is worth **£40billion!** Do you understand? **FORTY-BILLION-POUNDS!**" He gave a sardonic smile before adding, "that's at least five times more money than your parents ever had."

"You'll never be worth anywhere near what Mr and Mrs Hamley were!" cried Mo, sobbing uncontrollably on the floor. "You are a terrible, awful man Mike, you're not fit to carry the Hamley name!"

"My brother and his wife were foolish people!" cried Mike, bitterness sweeping his face. "They gave all their money to charity, to stupid pathetic polar bears, elephants and homeless people!" He slung his arms in disgust. "All the while I've had to spend years scrimping and saving to get by!"

"What?" wailed Mo incredulously. "They bought you a house *and* a penthouse apartment! They paid off all of your debts! Bought you a car! A motorbike! Paid for you to go to university. Paid for all of your holidays!" She paused for a moment. "They even paid for the operation to make your nose less pointy!"

"His nose was even pointier than that?" scoffed Mr Howler. "Crikey, you could sharpen a pencil with that thing!

The hostages laughed. So did Gruff. Terry put his head down when Mike looked at him.

"And don't forget my Mum and Dad gave you a job to run their company!" cried Ben, shaking with a mix of anger and sadness.

"And he made a mess of that!" mocked Mr Owen.

"I don't care about any of that," said Mike calmly. "Because now, I am rich beyond my wildest dreams! I can do what I want, when I want, wherever I want, and no one can stop me! Come on Terry, let's get out of here."

And with that, Mike and Terry began to edge away. Their faces disappearing in the faded light as they slowly stepped backwards with their guns trained on Gruff and the hostages. Ben, meanwhile, still tied up with the others, started to worry as a thought entered his head; what will Gruff do now? He has no diamond, no money, and no friends. He's likely to be very angry which doesn't bode well. At least he didn't have a gun. Just as Mike and Terry were about to disappear from view, the lights came on suddenly. Everyone flinched in the sudden brightness. "Who's that?" called Terry, visibly frightened. Suddenly, Terry and Mike were engulfed by a supersized net that landed on top of them from above. They tried to break free, but they were trapped. They started firing their guns in blind panic.

BANG! BANG! BANG!

The hostages tried their best to shuffle out of harm's way. Ben glanced up and unbeknown to Mike and Terry, behind them was a group of men who Ben had never seen before. Like special agents, they expertly jumped on Mike and Terry, who were wriggling around in the net like freshly caught fish. They quickly wrestled them into submission and removed their guns.

"Who are they?" asked Ben, his heart pounding.

"They're my friends," smiled Hannah. "From the streets, you kindly gave us somewhere to sleep tonight."

"Yes young man, good job!" winked Tony. "That's what happens in life when you are kind to people!"

"Oi Gruff! Come back!" bellowed Mr Howler.

While Mike and Terry were caught up in the net, Gruff was trying to make his getaway. He panted heavily as he ran down the dinosaur aisle, away from the homeless heroes.

"When will this ever end?" sighed Mrs Chopra. "Can't we just catch them all at the same time?"

Tony smiled. "I think we just have, look..."

With perfect timing, the police arrived. Blue lights flashed outside the store and the place was soon swarming with activity. After being held hostage for almost three hours, Ben, Mo, Tony, Penelope, Vince, Mr Howler, Mrs Chopra and Mr Owen were untied along with Cyril and Hannah. Ben breathed a sigh of relief, more from finally being rid of the rubber snakes than anything else. "We're not selling these things in here anymore!" he laughed as he tossed them to the ground. He approached Mo and put his arms around her. She was the most important person in his life now and as he held her tight, he felt her whole body shaking from shock. Paramedics arrived at the scene and took Mo and Tony to hospital.

All the while, it took four police officers to wrestle Gruff to the ground. "GET OFF ME YA' FILFFY PIGS!" he screamed as he tried his best to fight back. After covering the poor police officers in spit from yelling and bawling the gangster was eventually handcuffed and dragged with Mike and Terry into a police van outside.

It was finally over.

Chapter Forty Five

“Now where were we?” smiled Ben.

The boardroom burst into laughter. It was two weeks later, and with Gruff, Terry and Mike in jail, this was the first time that the former hostages had been reunited. Once Tony and Mo had been treated for shock in hospital, and had returned home for some well-deserved rest, Ben’s mind was immediately focussed on saving Toy Co. His parents famous toy store was still in trouble and with Christmas just six weeks away, Ben was itching to get back down to business. So he had called the directors for an extraordinary board meeting; joining Mr Howler, Mrs Chopra and Mr Owen were Tony, Mo, Penelope, Vince, Cyril and Hannah.

“Now, if I could finally finish my presentation,” smiled Ben, wearing a brand new suit and tie. “Tony, please could you do the honours?”

“A pleasure boss,” winked Tony. He switched on the computer and a presentation appeared on the projector screen.

OPERATION 'SAVE TOY CO'

Ben smiled, "thank you Tony. Now, over the last five years, toys have changed dramatically. They have become more high-tech. They have got bigger - more life-like. But when you examine sales figures, you will actually see that children are buying less toys than ever before." To prove his point, Ben flicked the slides to display a graph on the big screen.

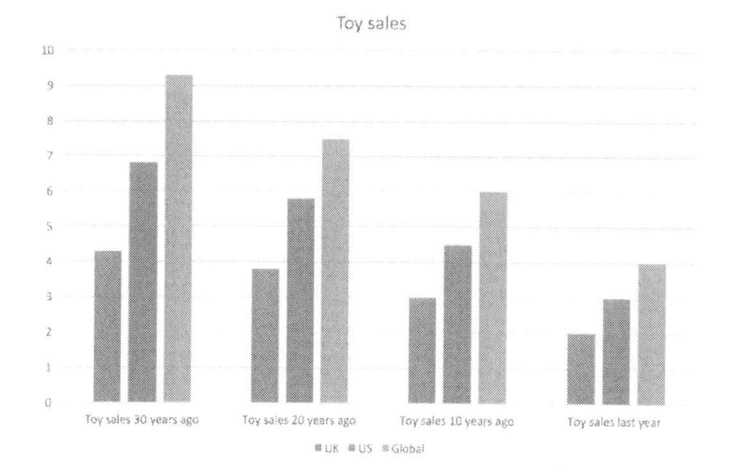

Ben stood up and began pacing the room. "And do you know why ladies and gentlemen? Do you know why children are buying less toys?"

The adults remained silent as they looked to one other for an answer.

"Well let me tell you," said Ben, his voice firm. "Children are buying less toys because they have lost the magic." He sat back down at the head of the table, perched higher now that Tony had fitted a booster seat! "Toys have lost the emotional connection. They are too complicated. Too many bits. Too many moving parts. There's no heart and soul in toys!" he cried, slamming his fist on the table before saying gently, "and we all know what children love more than anything in the whole world?"

There was a moment of silence.

"A hug!" wailed Ben, leaping from his chair. "All children love a nice cuddle from someone they love."

Vince and his Dad smiled at each other.

Ben went on, "and children love to use their imagination, we don't need to be given toys that do everything for us! We want to make them do the things that we want them to do!" Ben was on a roll now. "So I would like Toy Co to go back to basics. To go back to what we do best and make high quality toys that are honest and loveable - that last forever and can be passed down through generations." He paused as he popped open his briefcase and held up what appeared to be a very old and worn cuddly toy. "See this, this is 'Effervescent Elephant', which I took everywhere with me…" He cleared his throat, "until only recently…you see...I'm a bit too old now for a cuddly toy," he smiled bashfully. "My Dad made this when him and Mum founded Toy Co twenty years ago. It's timeless!" The directors nodded in approval. There were a few tears around the table as Ben continued, "now, the one thing that really sets this company apart from other toy stores is our work with charities. My parents have done so much to support vulnerable people and animals around the world. So…" The young boy paused before taking deep breath, "…in memory of my Mum and Dad, I am proud to present to you..." He pressed a button on the keyboard and a new slide displayed on the big screen which read 'Save the Endangered'

He stood tall and proud as he continued his presentation, "ladies and gentleman, I present to you 'Save the Endangered', a collection of high quality cuddly toys of animals at risk of extinction with 10% of profits going to save these beautiful creatures."

Flicking through the presentation slides as he introduced each animal, Ben's face glowed as he described each beautifully created design in detail. The directors looked on awe-inspired at the life-like designs of seven animals that are very sadly close to dying out. Each had their own unique and special characteristics which made them instantly loveable and huggable.

Save the Endangered comprised of a wise and super-intelligent Asian Elephant, a magnificently majestic Bengal Tiger, a great big Blue Whale, a cheeky Chimpanzee, a grumpy Gorilla, a playful Dolphin and finally, a dopy Penguin.

Ben went on, "these are premium teddies, of the very best quality. They will last a lifetime!" he announced passionately.

Mrs Chopra raised her hand. "Ben, this is a wonderful presentation. And the animals look absolutely fantastic. But please may I ask what they do?"

"Thank you Mrs Chopra. The animals don't do anything," smiled Ben.

"You mean they don't walk or move?" asked Mr Owen.

"Or talk?" asked Mr Howler.

"Nope. They don't do any of those things," said Ben, still smiling.

"So what you're saying is that the bears don't walk, talk, move, or make a sound?" asked Mr Howler.

"That's exactly what I'm saying," replied Ben.

The directors all looked at each other. There was a long period of silence before Mr Howler stood up and announced, "that is genius! Toys that don't do anything. I love it!" He began clapping passionately.

"Here here!" cheered the board.

Everyone stood up and clapped.

Ben's smile was as wide as the River Nile. "Thank you everyone," he beamed. "We have just six weeks until Christmas so let's get to work!

Chapter Forty Six

Rubbing his eyes, Ben woke up and glanced at the clock. It was just after 7am. He turned over and was about to go back to sleep when he suddenly remembered…

…IT WAS CHRISTMAS DAY!

He jumped out of bed, opened the curtains and was greeted by a truly spectacular view; like a glorious white carpet that glistened beautifully in the winter sun, his enourmous garden was covered in pristine snow, that gorgeous thick snow that crunches under your feet and makes the best kind of snowballs. Excited at the thought of getting out there on his sledge, he put his slippers on and pegged it downstairs. In the living room, sat in front of a roaring fire was Mo, wearing a festive dressing gown with reindeers on it and a smile as wide as Santa's belly. "Merry Christmas poppet," she said softly.

Ben ran towards her and gave her a hug. "Merry Christmas Auntie Mo," he said, nestling into her.

"I have a very special present for you," she whispered.

"What's that?" asked Ben. He joined his auntie on the sofa as she handed him an envelope. He opened it excitedly. What could be inside? His mood was quickly dampened when he discovered a letter with lots of writing and numbers. "What is it Mo?" he asked.

"Read it Ben," she said softly.

Before Ben could respond and remind her that he couldn't read it because he was dyslexic, his auntie put her arm around him and whispered, "poppet, just remember the techniques that we've used in the past. This is a letter that you'll want to read…go on…you can do it...I know you can…"

Ben focused on the letter. It looked impossibly hard to read but he suddenly remembered how he had gotten through all of those painful exams to get into King Admiral. Remembering what Mo and his parents had told him, about how to break words up into segments and to train his eyes across the page slowly, Ben read the letter out loud…

FAO: Ben Hamley, CEO Toy Co

Dear Ben,

I am writing to you with some rather splendid news. I have just received the Christmas sales figures. I am delighted to confirm that the Save the Endangered toy collection has sold 10,127,009 teddy bears in the Christmas sales period from 1 December to 23 December. Further information including the sales figures for each of the seven animals is listed on the next page but taking into account taxes and the 10% charitable donation for each bear sold, the profit from the Save the Endangered toy collection is estimated to be in the region of £54million. In addition, around £6million will be donated to charities to save these magnificent creatures.

As someone who has managed your late parents' wealth, business, and legal affairs since they founded Toy Co twenty years ago, I can safely say that this is the biggest selling toy in the history of the company! In fact, it has also been confirmed as the biggest selling toy of Christmas this year in the whole world.

You have saved Toy Co; your parents will be very proud of you - we are all proud of you.

Merry Christmas!

Your sincerely

Penelope Weston

Lawyer, Accountant, and coffee expert

In silence, Ben placed the letter on the coffee table. He put his head in his hands and began to cry softly.

"Oh Ben, whatever is the matter?" asked Mo, hugging him tightly.

Without lifting his head, the young boy wailed suddenly, "I wish Mum and Dad we're here!" He buried his head in Mo's super soft dressing gown and cried for the first time since his Mum & Dad had passed away three months ago. It was a very long cry. The type of cry that peaks and troughs, that lifts and lulls, that hurts and soothes, that can go from quiet sobbing to heavy wailing in an instant and then back again. Curled up into a ball on the sofa, young Benjamin Hamley cried his little heart out as he huddled into Mo who naturally joined in the crying marathon. There were wails, sighs, huffs, chuckles, groans, growls, sobs, and plenty of tears from the pair. You see, people deal with grief in all manner of ways. Like Mo, some find it easy to cry. Others like to get on with life and move on in the hope that the pain will eventually fade away. That is true to a certain extent, but the grief will always be there until you deal with it. If you don't acknowledge the need to grieve, it can manifest itself in other ways such as anger, frustration, or feeling sad for long periods of time.

After an hour of crying, at which point Mo's dressing gown was soaking wet with Ben's tears (and her own), the young boy finally sat up and rubbed his eyes. "I think I needed that!" he said with a hybrid chuckle and sob.

Mo took him by the hand and said, "oh Ben, your Mum and Dad would be so proud of you. Like you wouldn't believe. You have been through so much these last few months and you've dealt with it all so well." Tears formed in her eyes again. "You are such a special boy Ben Hamley."

"You certainly are Ben," came a voice.

Ben looked up and saw Tony, his warm smile making him immediately feel safe. "Good morning Tony, Merry Christmas!"

"And Merry Christmas to you young man," smiled Tony, donning a matching dressing gown to Mo.

“How about we all have a nice breakfast and a cup of tea? Chocolate spread on fresh bread?” smiled Mo, giving Tony a kiss on the cheek.

“That sounds just wonderful darling,” cooed Tony.

Watching Tony and Mo together made Ben’s heart fill with warmth and happiness. It is funny how life can turn out. Through his sheer determination to save Toy Co, Ben’s way of blocking out the loss of his parents, he had met Tony. And he introduced Tony to Mo. And now Tony and Mo had fell in love. It was truly fitting that two wonderful and kind people who had both lost their loved ones in the past, were now getting the best Christmas present they could ever wish for - a second chance of love. Not only that, Ben almost felt like he had a family again with Tony and Mo and that was the best Christmas present he could ever wish for.

“Come on then, let’s have breakfast,” whistled Mo. “Hannah and Vince will be round soon to play in the garden before Christmas dinner.”

The End

www.blossomspringpublishing.com